'So you came to Hooper to hide,' Nick stated.

'To sort myself out,' Rachel corrected.

'We can't fix every medical condition,' he said. 'It's unfortunate, but you have to accept that fact.'

She offered him a tremulous smile. 'My head agrees with you but my heart doesn't. And I don't know what to do about it.'

'The cure for falling off a horse is to get back on.'

He made it sound so easy, but it wasn't. 'What if I fall off again? What if someone else I know comes into ER and I freeze again?'

'And what if you don't?' he countered.

Rachel crossed her arms, feeling cold in spite of the temperature. 'I can't risk it. I won't.'

'You can't run forever.'

NURSES WHO DARE

The Wyman sisters—
women who conquer their fears and emotions
and win the lives and loves they long for.

In A NURSE'S FORGIVENESS Marta Wyman must
find it in her heart to forgive her grandfather for the act
that estranged him from her mother before Marta was
born. Dr Evan Gallagher is in New Hope to persuade
her to forgive and forget—especially as it becomes
clear that they can't be together until she does.

In A NURSE'S PATIENCE Amy loves her job
as a nurse-practitioner until Dr Ryan Gregory
joins the practice and questions her abilities.
She asks to work with another physician—
patience not being her strong point. But if she persists
she'll earn Ryan's trust and much, much more!

In A NURSE'S COURAGE Rachel Wyman
must find the courage to go back to the nursing
profession she loves after she is robbed of her
confidence when she is unable to help a dying friend.
Physician Nicholas Sheridan is the man to help her
rebuild her life. If she can find the courage
she'll not only win his trust, but his love.

A NURSE'S COURAGE

BY
JESSICA MATTHEWS

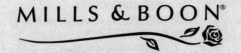

MILLS & BOON®

To Ryan, Tara, Erica, Avry, Adam and Casey. May you
face every situation with courage and a sense of humour.

To Martha Bross and Veda Boyd Jones
for your invaluable help with the local terrain.
Thanks for answering my last-minute questions.

*First published in Great Britain 2002
Harlequin Mills & Boon Limited,
Eton House, 18-24 Paradise Road, Richmond, Surrey TW9 1SR*

© Jessica Matthews 2002

ISBN 0 263 83059 4

*Set in Times Roman 10 on 11¼ pt.
03-0402-52658*

*Printed and bound in Spain
by Litografia Rosés, S.A., Barcelona*

CHAPTER ONE

'IS THERE a doctor or nurse in the building?'

Standing in the middle of the paint aisle at Bates' Lumber and Hardware Store, Rachel Wyman tensed. Couldn't fate let her lick her wounds in peace?

Apparently not, she thought wearily. So much for thinking that a small town several hundred miles from her old stomping grounds would have insulated her from her nursing profession.

Her *former* profession.

Even as she corrected herself, the irony of the situation struck her. She'd turned in her ID badge to her director of nursing and symbolically hung up her stethoscope a mere twenty-four hours ago. The ink probably hadn't even dried on her personnel file's 'Inactive' stamp and here she was, being called to serve in a career that she'd recently found unbearable.

The little voice in her head taunted her. *You don't have to go. You're not a nurse anymore, remember? No one will know.*

I will, her heart responded.

What good can you do? her alter ego whispered.

'Please report to the garden department immediately.'

The second announcement somehow caused her heart to overrule her mind, and she found herself heading toward the east end of the building. She should have chosen another place to pass the time until she could meet her grandmother, but she hadn't, and although she didn't want to feel the tug of duty, she did. With any luck, someone else was already administering first aid, which was probably all that was required any way.

Maybe it's more than that.

Be quiet, she ordered her little voice. Stop thinking of a worst-case scenario.

Her admonition was easier said than done. Considering her presence in the middle of a business geared to the home-do-it-yourselfer, it didn't take any effort to imagine a gruesome picture. During her career, she'd seen enough life-threatening injuries involving tools, wood or steel to fill a medical manual.

Those memories made it even more imperative to put aside her fears and act like a professional. For all of her shortcomings, she could easily be the only one who stood between a successful outcome or a tragedy. She'd never forgive herself if some hapless employee or customer died because of inadequate medical care. Her shoulders already carried a ton of guilt and couldn't handle one ounce more.

At that moment, her mind reluctantly admitted what her heart—and her feet—already knew. She couldn't ignore this summons any more than she could flap her arms and fly. However, that didn't mean she wouldn't defer to anyone else who had the slightest bit of emergency training.

Inhaling sharply, she almost expected to smell the familiar scent of hospital disinfectant. Instead, she recognized the distinctive aromas of paint and sawdust before she quickened her pace.

The absence of customers caught her notice as she traveled through the aisles, as did the childish screams in the background. The closer she got, the louder they became, and she forcibly squared her shoulders and deafened her ears. After everything that had happened in the last month, she dreaded dealing with children. Then again, she didn't look forward to dealing with adults either.

Rachel nudged her way into the small group of bystanders and employees who clogged the aisle while they murmured amongst themselves. Ghouls, every one of them, she thought crossly.

'Let me through, please,' she ordered. They apparently

heard her authoritative tone because they moved aside without question.

As soon as she'd run the gauntlet of spectators, she saw a tow-headed boy in green shorts and a T-shirt lying on the floor between a row of lawnmowers and a rack of yard tools. A wooden-handled rake lay across his body at a ninety-degree angle, its tines embedded along the length of his bare thigh.

A brunette who, based upon her anguish-furrowed face and red-rimmed eyes, was probably his mother knelt beside him on the concrete while a little girl looked over her shoulder in fear. Two store employees—a teenager and a middle-aged fellow—in their distinctive red vests hovered as well, their own distress mirrored on their faces.

Rachel sank to her knees beside the youngster. 'Has anyone called an ambulance?'

The older man whose name tag identified him as Bob Myles, Garden Department Manager, seemed relieved by the calm efficiency in her voice. 'Yes. They'll be here as soon as they can but they're on another call. Is there anything we should do for him in the meantime?'

'Just keep him quiet and clear the area.' Before she could tell the crowd to step back, a male voice rose above the background mutters of the spectators.

'OK, everyone. The show's over. Go on about your business.'

Rachel glanced in the direction of the newcomer. The mob parted like the Red Sea, revealing a dark-haired man she hadn't seen since the summer she'd turned seventeen, a man who possessed the brownest eyes and the boyishly handsome features she'd never expected to clap eyes on again.

Nicholas Sheridan.

She froze for a split second, meeting his gaze momentarily before she broke eye contact. Had he caught enough of a glimpse to recognize her? She prayed not. Returning to Hooper with her once-bright future burned out like an old light bulb was difficult enough, without running into someone who had success following him like a shadow.

Before she could finish her silent plea for anonymity, the manager broke in. 'Dr Sheridan.' The relief in his voice matched the expression on the boy's mother's face. 'Am I glad to see you.'

Doctor? Nicholas Sheridan had become a *doctor*? The information made Rachel all the more intent on blending into the background and she made a point of focusing on their young victim rather than the physician.

'Good thing I dropped by for nails.' Nick crouched at her side and gazed down at the youngster, shaking his head in the process. 'What happened to my old buddy, Kevin?'

'Don't forget to add "this time",' Kevin's mother said, sounding somewhat resigned.

'My week wouldn't be complete if I didn't see someone from the Pearson family in my office or in the ER.' Between his presence and his lighthearted voice, everyone's tension visibly eased. Kevin's mother had lost her frantic expression, as had the store's staff.

'Now, let's see the damage,' he said.

Instantly, their patient let out a howl. 'Don't touch it,' Kevin screamed.

'I won't,' Nick soothed. 'I'm just looking. Lie still for me, OK?'

Anticipating Nick's request, Rachel motioned to the teenage employee. Out of long habit, she murmured an order so as not to interrupt the physician's conversation. 'We need a first-aid kit and something to use as a splint. Several sturdy sticks or—'

'Will a board work?'

She smiled at him. 'Perfect. No more than two feet long, though.'

While the employee—Brad, according to his name badge—dashed away, she watched Nick conduct his examination with an unsurprisingly gentle technique. In sports, he'd possessed what people referred to as good hands, but his talent hadn't only lain on the basketball court or baseball field. He'd possessed an innate sense of touch, regardless of whether he'd been wielding a hammer or a screwdriver, or moving a bird's nest to a safer tree branch. Becoming a physician hadn't been such a far-fetched idea after all.

'Did you trip?' she heard him ask the little boy.

At Kevin's tearful nod, his mother declared, 'I warned them not to run, but do they listen?' She glared at her daughter who had the grace to appear thoroughly cowed by the damage their disobedience had caused.

Rachel took pity on Kevin's sister, with her two missing front teeth, baseball T-shirt, ragged red shorts and scraped knees. She possessed all the earmarks of being a tomboy, and an enthusiastic one, to boot.

'At least it was a clean rake,' she soothed, forgetting her wish to be invisible in order to console the family. Making accusations and placing blame wouldn't change the situation. First, they had to deal with the injury. 'It could be much worse, you know. He could have punctured his chest or his abdomen, or lost an eye.'

The woman's eyes widened as she realized the truth to Rachel's statement. Although the scene appeared like one from a horror movie, the bleeding was minimal and Rachel hoped the current status wouldn't change even though they were fortunate enough to have a doctor present.

'We'll need something to immobilize his leg and stabilize the rake head,' Nick mentioned.

'They're on their way,' Rachel answered crisply. She'd hardly finished speaking before Brad returned, out of breath but carrying a two-by-four inch board and first-aid kit triumphantly.

Rachel took the items and dug in the kit for a length of bandage, aware of Nick's gaze following her every move.

'I'm impressed,' he said softly. 'You're one step ahead of me.'

Ordinarily, satisfaction would have seeped through every

corner of her soul. Now, however, she only wanted to re-
treat to her own corner.

'I'll get out of your way, Doctor,' she said politely, holding out a length of brown elastic wrap, 'so you can take
over.'

He placed a hand on her shoulder and ignored her offering. 'Don't go. Several pairs of hands will come in
handy.'

She sank onto her heels again, disappointed by her foiled
escape plan.

'How are you doing, sport?' he asked Kevin.

Kevin sniffled. 'Not…not so good.'

'You'll be better before long,' Nick promised. 'I know
your leg hurts, but we'll give you something as soon as we
get more help. Can you hang tough for a little longer?'

'I…I'll try.'

He patted Kevin's arm. 'Good boy. Have you ever ridden
in an ambulance?'

The youngster shook his head.

'Then you'll have your first trip today. Your friends will
be so jealous.'

He motioned to the lawnmowers and yard tools surrounding them. 'Any chance we can move these things?
We're going to need elbow room.'

Immediately, Bob and Brad began moving the merchan-
dise. The unmistakable sounds of equipment being dragged
across the concrete floor and metal grating on metal rang
in Rachel's ears as she laid a roll of gauze next to the board
lying near Kevin's injured leg.

'Have you done this before?' Nick asked.

'No,' she said honestly. She usually stood on the receiving end of an emergency and not the shipping end, but she
purposely didn't explain.

'You have had medical training, though,' he stated, as if
only waiting for her to confirm what he'd already guessed.

'Some.' Rachel rummaged in the kit for adhesive tape,
grateful for the task that kept her from meeting Nick's gaze.

Perhaps she was being petty for not revealing her nurse's training, but if she did, an inevitable onslaught of questions would follow. It would be far better if he simply thought she'd taken a first-aid course.

'You seem familiar,' he mentioned offhandedly. 'Any connections to Kansas City?'

Her lungs seemed to stop functioning. If only the ambulance crew would arrive…. 'No.'

To Rachel's relief, Brad joined their small circle and interrupted their conversation. 'Aren't you going to pull the rake out of his leg?'

Kevin whimpered and Nick laid a reassuring hand on the boy's shoulder. 'Absolutely not. We'll let the surgeon do the honors under more controlled circumstances. We don't know what damage has been done and I don't want to cause more.' He glanced up from his task. 'We'll need to either remove or shorten the handle, though.'

'Why?' Brad asked, plainly curious.

'He'll be easier to transport,' Nick replied. 'There'll be less risk of the ambulance crew dislodging the tines while they're moving him.'

'Oh.'

'I'll have someone bring a power saw,' the manager said. 'We have one that goes through wood like a hot knife through butter.'

Rachel heard the boast in his voice and was certain he'd recited part of his sales pitch. Within seconds of his comment, he went to a phone strategically placed under an overhang, dialed a number and barked out his request.

'We'll need a blanket or a drop cloth to cover him, too,' Nick called out.

The manager acknowledged Nick's request with a wave of his hand as he continued to speak into the receiver.

'It's gonna hurt, isn't it?' Kevin's lower lip trembled and tears began flowing down his face.

'We're going to be very careful,' Rachel assured him.

On Nick's count of three, he raised the boy's leg high

enough for Rachel to slide the board underneath. Between
the two of them, they immobilized his leg with the elastic
wrap.

'You really are good,' he said as he continued to hold
the board so Rachel could wind gauze around the impale-
ment site. 'Not too tight and not too loose.'

'Thanks.'

'New in town?' he asked.

'More or less.'

'Are you looking for a job?'

'No,' she answered instantly. 'I have one.' To her relief,
the emergency medical team arrived and the conversation
that had strayed too close to her personal life ended
abruptly.

Sensing that Kevin's sister needed a reassuring hug,
Rachel pulled her aside. They watched while an EMT covered Nick, Kevin and his mother with a sheet of plastic.

'Why are they putting plastic over them?' she wanted to
know.

'To protect them from flying wood chips and sawdust,'
Rachel answered. One of the men revved up the saw, but
luckily the roar was blessedly brief.

'What's your name?' Rachel asked.

'Sunny. It's short for Sonja, but I like Sunny better.'

Rachel loosely held Sunny's fingers while they watched
Nick and the ambulance crew prepare Kevin for transport.
Because Nick appeared so engrossed in his patient, Rachel
felt safe to study him, albeit surreptitiously.

Most things about him hadn't changed since their last
summer together. His hair color had remained the same nut-
brown shade and his dark eyes still glittered with a sparkle
that turned average features into handsome ones. He'd always been tall for his age, as had she, but some time during
the intervening years the height difference had grown sig-
nificantly. Plus, he'd filled out, developing a muscular phy-
sique that made him a breathtakingly attractive man in
faded blue jeans and a snug gray T-shirt. If he looked this

good in old clothes, he'd be a real ladykiller when he dressed for a special occasion.

Father Time had definitely improved upon what Mother Nature had given.

Rachel suddenly felt self-conscious. How could fate possibly have allowed his path to cross hers at this particular moment in her life? The same man who didn't understand or include the word 'failure' in his vocabulary?

He hadn't been malicious, but teasing her had been his favorite pastime when they'd been younger and she could easily imagine how he'd rub her nose in her shortcomings now. He'd outdone her at everything, from climbing trees to earning money at their curbside lemonade stand. He was the best of the best and he both expected and inspired the same out of everyone else.

He wouldn't get it from her, she thought. She'd already seen how her best had fallen short and now she had nothing left to give.

The men bundled Kevin onto the stretcher and locked the wheels in place. Sunny tugged Rachel's hand. 'Is he gonna be OK?'

Rachel felt reasonably safe in answering, 'Absolutely. He'll be chasing after you before you know it.' Seeing Sunny's mother glance around, presumably in search of her daughter, Rachel released her. 'Looks like your mom is ready to go.'

Sunny rushed to her parent's side, then turned and waved.

Rachel smiled and gave her the thumbs-up sign, grateful for the end of her part in this little drama. The emergency medical team had momentarily diverted Nick's attention, so it seemed the perfect time to escape. In a few weeks, after she'd settled into her new routine and recharged her mental batteries, she'd be ready to renew old acquaintances, but not today.

She spotted her purse off to one side where someone—probably Brad—had moved it out of the way. Silently and without any lingering glances, she slung it over her left shoulder and walked toward the side exit.

Before she could push open the glass door, the sound of her name halted her in her tracks.

'Rachel!'

Caught off guard, she whirled and found Nick staring at her. His expression was unreadable, but his eyes held the glimmer of recognition.

'Don't leave,' he ordered. 'I want to talk.' Before she could answer or check her watch to see if she was overdue in meeting her grandmother, he turned away to speak to the EMTs.

Dear Lord, he'd recognized her! Once again, she railed against fate as a familiar feeling of dread swept over her. However, as the minutes ticked by with not a glance in her direction, anger replaced her alarm.

How typical of him to deliver instructions and expect her to follow them, she thought peevishly. She had better things to do than wait for him indefinitely, especially as she didn't want to speak to him in the first place. Nick may have ordered her around when they were kids and he might issue commands to his subordinates at the hospital, but she didn't fit into either of those categories now.

Nick Sheridan would simply have to wait until she squeezed him into *her* schedule.

She turned on one heel and strode through the exit into the sun-baked parking lot.

She'd walked out on him.

The notion plagued Nick Sheridan from the time the EMTs loaded Kevin in the ambulance until he spoke to the nurse on the pediatrics wing of Hooper General where Kevin would return after his stint in the recovery room.

He still couldn't believe Rachel had pulled such a fast and effective disappearing act. One minute, she'd been standing off to the side, keeping company with Kevin's sister. The next, she was gone. After asking her to stay, he couldn't believe she'd vanished.

If she was meeting someone, she could have said so, he thought, although he realized that he hadn't given her the opportunity. Yet something didn't ring true about the situation. Rachel hadn't acted pleased to see him and had appeared even less thrilled to remain. He tried to remember if they'd parted years ago under a cloud, but he immediately dismissed the idea. Rachel wasn't the type to hold a grudge, much less hold one for this long.

Maybe she was upset because he hadn't instantly recognized her, but surely she couldn't blame him. She'd changed a lot over the years. The gangly girl had developed into a curvaceous woman, her face now showed the delicate angles of high cheekbones, contacts had obviously replaced the chunky plastic-framed eyeglasses, and her voice had become more husky. Her vibrant hair color, however, had remained the same. The distinct hue had been the key characteristic which had enabled him to identify her.

At first, he'd thought she'd forgotten him—a notion that had pricked his ego mightily—but then she hadn't seemed surprised when he'd called her by name.

Something, maybe even *someone*, was bothering her. He knew it as well as he knew his address and phone number. He'd always been able to read people fairly accurately, and his senses in that regard had grown rather than diminished.

Frustrated by his inability to understand Rachel's actions and to reach anyone at the Wymans' home, he spoke sharply to Hope Maxwell, a seasoned nurse in her fifties who protected her patients' interests as well as her own family's. At the moment, she appeared haggard and worn.

'Why isn't the latest temperature recorded for the Jackson girl? It's supposed to be charted every hour.'

Hope dug in her pocket for her notes. 'Because I haven't had a free moment,' she retorted before she read off the number. 'Be glad I squeezed in time to take it in the first place. We're short-staffed today.'

'Again?' He shoved thoughts of Rachel aside and focused on an issue that was fast becoming a major problem—their nursing shortage.

'Again?' she asked, in disbelief. 'Haven't you heard it's
standard operating procedure these days? Even ICU isn't
faring any better.'

Nick muttered a curse under his breath. 'Doesn't Administration know this is a lawsuit waiting to happen?'

Hope shrugged. 'Far be it for me to figure out their
minds. I'm low man on the totem pole. Besides, if I don't
see some relief soon, I'm moving into another line of work.
I didn't sign on to bear the brunt of everyone's complaints
because I can't be in three places at once. I never thought
I'd say this, but my job satisfaction level is sinking like a
cement block in a pond.'

Nick drew a deep breath. 'Sorry. I know it's not your
fault. *Darn fools*,' he muttered under his breath.

'Did you need anything else?' Hope asked.

'When Recovery brings the Pearson boy here, do your
best to keep him occupied. He's a real livewire.'

'I'll try, but I can only do so much.'

'I know. Do what you can.' He turned to leave, then
stopped. 'Has the rumor mill said anything about the hospital hiring any new nursing staff?'

'Not that I've heard. Why?'

'No reason,' he said, unwilling to put his suspicions into
words yet.

'If you find another nurse, I certainly hope you'll steer
her in our direction.'

'I'll do my best.'

Disappointed by Hope's inability to shed any light on
Rachel's job, he headed for the first floor and the doctors'
entrance located near the ER. As he sailed through the now
quiet department, he saw Dylan Gower, the weekend con-
tract ER physician, leaning back in his chair behind the
nurses' station counter with his hands clasped behind his
head, a picture of ease.

A few years older than Nick, Dylan had sandy-colored hair and wore rimless glasses. Because he worked from Friday evening until Monday morning, people rarely saw him in anything other than green scrubs and a white lab coat.

'What's the rush?' Dylan asked.

Nick slowed, somewhat chagrined that his eagerness to track down Rachel showed. 'No reason.'

'I don't blame you for wanting to get out of here. It's too nice a day to spend it in this sterile environment. What do you have planned?'

Nick veered toward the desk and rested his forearms on the chest-high counter above the desk. 'I'm looking for someone.'

Dylan grinned. 'Must be a woman.'

'What makes you say that?'

'We've already handled the emergency, so what else could it be? You should leave a few of the single gals for the rest of us bachelors, you know.'

Nick laughed. 'It wouldn't do any good, old buddy. You can't go out while you're on duty and you don't stay in town the rest of the week.'

'I would be if I had someone to stay in town for.'

'Yeah, right,' Nick scoffed. 'Says the original Dr Workaholic. For your information, I'm trying to find an old friend.'

'The gal at the hardware store?'

Nick narrowed his eyes. 'Yeah. How did you know?'

Dylan guffawed. 'Those EMTs sang like canaries in exchange for our leftover morning donuts. I hear she's quite the looker.'

'She's pretty,' Nick agreed, playing down his opinion. 'Above average height, short brown hair, dark eyes.' If he mentioned how her curly hair had enough strands of red to remind him of a sorrel's coat, and how her brown eyes matched the color of the thick, rich molasses that her grandmother used in her famous gingerbread, Dylan would have accused him of waxing poetic and Nick would never hear the end of his friend's teasing.

'Sounds like half the female population. Any distinguishing features? Like a wedding ring?'

'No.' In fact, she hadn't worn a ring of any kind.

'Where are you meeting her?'

'I'm not,' Nick admitted. 'She left before I could talk to her.'

'I wouldn't take it personally,' Dylan said. 'Maybe she had an appointment.'

'She could have said so.'

'Then call her.'

'I would, if I knew where she was staying.' He was ninety-nine per cent certain she would be at Hester's and Wilbur's house but, without an answering machine, he couldn't leave a message.

'She said she has a job,' Nick continued. 'You haven't heard of any new nurses being hired, have you?'

Dylan shook his head. 'I'm usually the last one to find out, but if you haven't heard from her in ages, what makes you think she's a nurse?'

'I'm not positive but, after seeing her in action with the Pearson kid, and knowing how she had an interest in nursing at one time, I'd say the odds were good.'

'If she's working here, you can easily track her down. Check with Personnel on Monday.'

'I will.' He would, too, provided he couldn't locate her in the meantime. 'I just can't understand why she didn't wait when I'd asked her to.' Neither could he understand why she hadn't acknowledged him after Bob had greeted him, or been more forthcoming about her medical training.

'Women.' Dylan shrugged and threw up his hands. 'Who can figure them out? Maybe your Florence Nightingale didn't want to run into you.'

His colleague's comment confirmed what Nick had already suspected. Rachel had avoided meeting his gaze while they'd helped Kevin Pearson. His gut told him that

she would have disappeared after Brad had brought the
first-aid kit if he'd given her the opportunity. Luckily, Nick
had asked for her help, otherwise he'd never have realized
who she was. For whatever reason, Rachel Wyman obviously didn't want a reunion.

Dylan stood. As he walked past Nick, he clapped him
on the back. 'I wouldn't worry about it. Most people don't
dress up when they're going to the hardware store. If she's
anything like my sisters, she probably wants to look her
best when she meets up with an old friend and swaps life
histories. You know how women are.'

Rachel may not have been wearing her Sunday best, but
Nick couldn't fault her appearance. She'd looked great in
her khaki shorts and a yellow top that had clung to her like
a second skin. *He* had been the one who'd looked like a
shady character in dust-covered jeans and a shrunken
T-shirt, not to mention his dire need for a haircut.

'You're probably right,' Nick answered, not totally convinced but unable to think of his own plausible explanation.

'I know I am. Now, I'm off to grab a few winks before
the Saturday night crowd turns this place into the hottest
spot in town.'

Nick headed for the parking lot, determined to drive to
the Wymans' home in search of Rachel. If she was indeed
a nurse, and she *wasn't* employed at Hooper General, he'd
rectify that as soon as possible. It was a sin to waste talent
like hers.

CHAPTER TWO

'I HATE to see you waste your ability, Rachel. It isn't too late to change your mind.'

Rachel hid her frustration over her grandmother's well-meant comment behind a tired half-smile. 'If I had a dollar for every time I heard someone tell me that,' she said lightly, 'I'd be an extremely rich woman.'

'I know, dear.' The seventy-two-year-old Hester patted Rachel's hand. 'I'd promised myself and your grandfather that I wouldn't say one word about your decision, and now I've gone and broken my vow already.'

Rachel hugged the petite woman who, other than her sisters, was all she had left of her parents, including her stepmother. 'Don't worry. I won't hold it against you.'

Hester pulled out of Rachel's embrace and held her at arm's length. 'It's just that we're concerned. You've always been so adaptable and enthusiastic.'

'I still am. I've simply switched gears.'

'Giving up your nursing career to renovate this house simply isn't like you.'

The idea hadn't ever occurred to Rachel either, until a month ago when her entire world had shifted and she'd lost her bearings. She'd learned one thing during the past four weeks and it was that nothing—no matter how hard one worked or planned—came with any guarantees. Plans were only dreams that had all the substance of the morning mist and were subject to the whims of drunk drivers and fatal illnesses.

'Trust me. I know what I'm doing.'

Something in her voice must have convinced her grandparent because Hester finally nodded. 'All right. I won't say another word. But you've seen my sister's house and the shape she left it in. If you should change your mind about updating it, your grandpa and I will understand.'

Renovating a hundred-year-old structure hadn't ever been on Rachel's things-to-do-in-her-lifetime list, but as soon as she'd seen it, surrounded by weeds and standing proudly in spite of its air of neglect and genteel poverty, she hadn't been able to imagine walking away. She understood how it felt—tired, run-down, battered by storms and violated by vandals. It seemed to reflect everything in her own life that had gone wrong. She felt a subtle link being forged between them, as if both she and the house shared a kindred spirit.

How appropriate for her to restore this house to its former glory. If only she could mend her own heartaches as easily.

'Remodeling will keep me busy,' she said, well aware of the enormity of the task. 'Which is what I need right now.'

'If you think so.' Hester cleared her throat. 'You haven't said how Charles is taking your decision.'

As a computer programmer, Charles was the head of her hospital's information system. They'd fallen into an easy relationship several years ago when he'd been involved in training the supervisory staff on the latest software upgrades. In the course of their week-long class, he'd discovered her appreciation for blue-grass music and had asked her to attend a festival where artists who specialized in that type of country music had performed. Gradually, they'd gone out more and more, eventually drifting together until they'd become known as a couple. He was sweet and kind and understanding, but somewhat absent-minded when he was involved in a project, which was most of the time.

How was Charles taking her decision? Unfortunately, she doubted if he'd remember she'd left town until their usual Thursday night date rolled around.

'He agrees I should get away for awhile,' she said. He'd seemed leery of her decision to quit her job, but overall he'd taken her announcement in his stride. True to form, he hadn't argued or tried to change her mind. Then again, she couldn't ever remember if he'd ever questioned her about anything. He allowed her to be truly independent.

'That's nice.' Hester's voice developed a brisk quality. 'I'd show you through the detached garage, but I promised to meet your grandfather and you know what a stickler for time he is.' She hesitated. 'Maybe I should have found a substitute for our weekly Pitch Club.'

'Don't be ridiculous.' Rachel ushered her grandmother through the dark, gloomy rooms and out the front door. 'I'll be fine. I'd prefer a quiet evening to settle in, anyway.'

'If you're sure…'

'I am.'

'The plumber is supposed to start work on Monday. You have running water, but I do wish Wilbur hadn't taken out the bathtub. Until it's replaced, you can shower at our house any time, day or night. I'm afraid, though, you'll find driving across town to be terribly inconvenient.'

'Inconvenience is part and parcel of any remodeling project. I'll cope.'

'The good thing is, you won't have to endure those arrangements for long.' Hester stepped onto the porch and paused. 'You have our phone number?'

'Next to the telephone,' Rachel assured her. 'If I need anything, I'll call. I promise.'

'And I gave you the keys.'

Rachel held up a large ring and jangled it. 'Thanks for marking which one goes with which lock.'

'Yes, well, your grandfather labeled those, so if you can't read his writing call him. There is one, though, he couldn't identify.'

'OK.' Determined to broach a certain subject before her grandmother sidetracked her again, Rachel said, 'By the way, I saw Nick Sheridan today.'

Her grandmother appeared startled. 'You did?'

'Yeah. I didn't realize he'd moved back or that he'd become a doctor.'

'He hasn't been here very long. Did he say anything to you?'

'Only hello.' Actually, he'd only said her name, but she spared Hester the details. 'We didn't have a chance to talk.'

'Well, I'm sure you'll run into him again, dear.' Hester moved toward the top step. 'I really must be going—'

'If he should call you, please, don't tell him where I am. I'm not in the mood for company.'

Hester's brow developed another wrinkle and her hand fluttered to her throat. 'What makes you think he'd call us?'

'He'll assume I'm staying with you. Let's keep it that way.'

'I know that you have never liked to talk about things that bothered you, at least not at first, but maybe Nick can help you regain your perspective.'

'I don't think so, Grams. Getting over Grace and Molly's...' She couldn't force herself to say the word 'deaths' so she substituted '...situation is something I have to do for myself. Please?'

Hester's shoulders slumped. 'All right. I won't say a word about you if he telephones us.' She waggled her fingers in a wave. 'We'll drop in tomorrow after church to check on you.'

While Hester carefully picked her way down the dry-rotted steps and hurried to her car, Rachel took a moment to shut her eyes and breathe deeply, imagining the scent of freshly cut grass, the fragrance of marigolds and the colorful backdrop of the purple petunias she intended to plant. Peace and quiet. The perfect prescription for what ailed her.

Immediately, Nick returned to her thoughts. Even if her grandmother kept her whereabouts quiet, Nick was determined enough to find her. The best she could hope for was a few days' reprieve before he appeared on her doorstep. Perhaps she should have stayed a little longer at the hardware store and made light conversation, but she hadn't. She'd probably wounded his pride but if he left her alone as a result, she wouldn't complain.

She smiled, wondering if Nick's ladykiller reputation remained intact. Grams had kept her informed of his high-school conquests, but the news had dropped off once he'd graduated and his mother had moved away. After seeing him work on the Pearson boy and noticing the absence of a wedding band, Rachel suspected that he hadn't committed himself to one woman yet. Knowing Nick, he probably never would.

A quiet sigh escaped her. She had more important things to think about than Nick Sheridan. Top on the list was her intention to make the house presentable for prospective buyers before the winter weather arrived and the housing market slowed. At least her Great-Aunt Matilda had possessed enough foresight to turn the space over the garage into an apartment. Renting those quarters would provide some income for her grandparents while she worked on the house they'd inherited.

Rachel trod lightly on the rickety steps and headed for the garage. Her grandmother hadn't mentioned if the furnished apartment was ready for someone to move in, but if it was, she'd advertise it in the classifieds on Monday.

She opened the door, made a mental note to take care of the squeak and stepped inside. The interior was as she'd expected—concrete floor, a workbench on one side and a pervasive odor of gasoline and oil. The steps leading upstairs were made of unfinished pine and stood directly in front of her. Without hesitation, she took them and soon found herself on a landing where another door barred her way. After finding the right key, the doorknob turned easily and she crossed the threshold.

Unlike the house, this area didn't have the same closed-in, musty smell. Obviously, her grandparents had aired and dusted it recently. An old sofa with bizarre gold and green upholstery and a square table with two rather uncomfort-able-looking metal dining chairs filled most of the space. The kitchenette was to the right and contained a hot plate, a small microwave and a dorm-room-sized refrigerator.

Of the two doors at the far end of the main living area, one opened into a tiny bathroom while a bedroom lay behind the second door. The furniture was old and showed signs of wear and a soft chenille spread covered the bed.

The sight reminded her of how long her day had already been. She'd gotten up before dawn to finish packing, driven for hours before arriving in Hooper, suffered through the episode at the hardware store and then toured her temporary home. She hadn't realized how daunting the task awaiting her was until she'd seen it up close and personal.

With all of that behind her, she couldn't resist the allure of the mattress. Her grandparents weren't hard enough task-masters to begrudge her a catnap on her first day in town.

Rachel climbed onto the right side, stretched out her weary bones and closed her eyes, vowing to unpack after a thirty minute break.

Lulled by the birds chirping in the tree outside her window, her thoughts wandered. She wouldn't miss the sound of cars careening down the street or sirens blaring at all hours of the day for one reason or another. In fact, she looked forward to putting prima donna physicians and tight-fisted administrators behind her in favor of a simpler lifestyle.

Idly, she wondered what kind of doctor Nick Sheridan had turned out to be. He hadn't seemed as arrogant as some she'd dealt with, but she couldn't tell after one encounter. Was he still the rascal who hid his single-minded determination underneath a layer of charm?

Probably so, she thought as drowsiness overtook her.

'And who is sleeping in *my* bed?'

The melodic tenor drawl roused her in time to notice a shadowy tall shape moving toward her. Her instincts, honed from living in the city, took over. She rolled across the bed to the opposite side, landed on her feet and drew back her arm to swing the pillow she'd grabbed.

'Whoa, there,' the man said, raising his hands. 'A little jumpy today, Rachel?'

Hearing her name spoken so familiarly was enough for her to shake off the last remnants of sleep fogging her brain.

She blinked, bringing her swimming contacts into focus, and gasped as she recognized the man she'd done her utmost to avoid.

Nick pointed to the pillow. 'I should warn you. If you're going to hit me, you might choose something that packs a little more punch.'

Rachel glanced down and realized how ridiculous she must appear waving her small pillow around. An embarrassed warmth spread over her face as she tossed it on the bed.

'I was making do with what I had,' she defended.

'I'm lucky you don't sleep with a baseball bat.'

'I may start,' she mumbled, sinking onto the bed and tucking her legs underneath her. Just a few minutes ago, she'd thought she'd have a few days' reprieve before she had to face him. Instead, she'd only gained a few hours.

'How did you find me?' she asked, certain of her grandmother's pledge of secrecy.

'You ran away,' he countered.

His inference was obvious. 'I waited as long as I could. I assumed you'd go to the hospital and we couldn't talk anyway.'

'I did. I only wanted to ask if you were going to be in town for a while and where I could reach you. We haven't seen each other in, what, ten years?'

'Twelve, but who's counting?' They'd both been juniors in high school when she'd spent her last summer in Hooper.

'You should have said something,' he chided. 'You had the advantage of knowing my name from the start. I had to figure out yours. You've changed.' He smiled. 'For the better, I might add.'

She may have changed a lot, and he had changed a little, but his grin remained the same. It still possessed enough power to make the recipient feel special. She should know. She'd seen his smile often enough and had developed a crush over him because of it. Unfortunately, she'd soon learned that she hadn't stood a chance against the rest of the girls in his line-up. After she'd accepted the fact, his teasing grin had become more of an irritant than a blessing.

Her skin warmed under his praise. 'Thanks. You're looking good yourself.'

'After I realized who you were,' he continued, 'I thought maybe you had forgotten me.'

She tugged on a tuft of chenille and avoided his gaze. 'I didn't. Standing over a kid with a rake in his leg just didn't seem the appropriate time to stage a reunion. How is he, by the way?'

'He's fine. Some muscle damage but, other than the unusual scars, he'll be tearing around his house again before long.'

'That's wonderful.'

His gaze grew intent. 'What brings you to Hooper?'

She recited her prepared response. 'I thought I should spend some time with my grandparents. They aren't getting any younger.'

'What have you been doing since I saw you last?'

'A little of this and that.'

'Oh, really?' He leaned against the doorframe and crossed his arms. 'What exactly is "this" and "that"?'

Rachel suddenly felt like she was being hunted. She'd learned long ago that in order to hold her own in any debates with Nick Sheridan, she had to keep her wits about her. At the moment, her physical and mental exhaustion made her a weak verbal sparring partner, and she wasn't about to divulge her past to someone who couldn't possibly understand her emotional turmoil.

'You didn't answer me earlier,' she reminded him, changing the subject. 'What are you doing here and how did you get in?'

'I could ask you the same question,' he drawled. 'For the record, you're in *my* room, Goldilocks.'

She shot him an exasperated glare. 'The fairy-tale name doesn't apply, and you know it.'

He grinned. 'You may not have golden hair, but I did find you sleeping in my bed.'

'You're mistaken,' she insisted. 'I just drove into town and I was checking out the apartment to see if it was ready to be rented.'

Nick straightened. 'It is. I'm the tenant and I have the keys to prove it.'

'You're joking.'

He dug in his pocket and jangled a keyring. 'Most furnished apartments don't include state-of-the-art stereo equipment or a television,' he pointed out. 'Or didn't you see those when you walked in? If you're still not convinced…' He motioned to the dresser across the room. '*My* clothes are in the drawers.'

Rachel glanced around the room, finally noticing what she hadn't seen upon entering. She'd been so tired and so delighted to see a bed that she hadn't noticed anything else.

A bottle of men's cologne, several newspapers, a small vial of acetaminophen and nail clippers lay on the embroidered dresser scarf. A book about Navy Seals lay on the opposing nightstand next to a pile of thrillers.

A spicy citrus scent hanging in the air confirmed his claim, but she wasn't ready to concede. She rose regally, stomped to the dresser and pulled out the top drawer, only to discover neat piles of colored socks and men's briefs. She slammed the drawer shut, placed her hands on the flat surface and hung her head.

Sweet Saints above! He was right. She *had* been sleeping in his bed. To make matters worse, she'd never be able to look at him without wondering about the color of his underwear.

Forcing herself to turn around, she faced him. 'I don't understand…'

Nick straightened, then approached the bed where he perched on the edge. 'It's simple really,' he said, patting a spot beside him.

She ignored his invitation to join him. 'I'm listening.'

'Hester inherited this property from her sister three months ago—'

'I'm well aware of my grandmother's circumstances.'

Nick shot her a let-me-finish look and she raised her hands.
'Sorry. Go ahead.'

'For the last ten years of her life, your Great-Aunt
Matilda let the place deteriorate. From what I understand,
vandals added to the results caused by nature and neglect.'

So far, he hadn't told her anything that she didn't already
know. Rachel narrowed her eyes. 'How do you fit into this
picture?'

'Your grandfather offered this apartment to me a month
ago when I moved to town. He asked if I'd help out with
some of the remodeling in exchange for rent.'

'Why you?' she asked, puzzled. 'You're a doctor. You
don't have time for this.'

'I have more than you think. We don't handle obstetrics
and I'm only on call every third evening and weekend. The
ER is staffed with a physician, so my call-backs are usually
minimal.'

'Yes, but how does being a physician qualify you to—?'

'I worked in construction to earn extra money during
college. Woodworking is my hobby. So what's your story?'

'Grams asked me to work on the house, too. I can't believe she didn't say anything about you being a part of this
project.'

He shrugged. 'Maybe she didn't think it was important.'

Rachel disagreed. Although she hadn't known of Nick's
arrival in Hooper, her grandmother surely would have
known that Nick fell under the heading of 'medical things
to avoid.' Now that she thought about it, Hester had acted
strangely after Rachel had requested her to keep her whereabouts a secret. Clearly, her grandmother knew that Rachel
would run into him before the day ended.

'Then working on the house is the job you'd mentioned?'
he asked.

'Yes.'

'How long are you planning to stay in Hooper?'

'I haven't decided. At least until the house is ready to
be sold.'

'And then what?' he pressed.

'Why the twenty questions?' she asked.

'Just trying to be friendly.'

'I'm not here to socialize.'

'As usual, Rachel has her nose to the grindstone,' he teased. 'You know, your grandparents may have thought two sets of hands were better than one. It certainly won't be as lonely.'

Disappointment welled inside her. So much for her plans for peace and quiet, for mind-numbing isolation, for an opportunity to rethink the direction of her life.

'I don't want to work with anyone,' she pointed out.

'To be honest,' he said, 'I'm not any happier about this development than you are.'

'Oh?'

'Admit it, Rach. You and I didn't always see eye to eye. If I suggested one thing, you insisted upon another. We couldn't even agree on the color of paint to use for the birdhouse we built.'

'You never asked my opinion. You dictated.'

'I usually had a better idea.'

She scoffed. 'Says you. In any case, our little disagreements never seemed to stop you from coming around to see me.'

He grinned. 'I guess they didn't. So, why do you want to tackle Hester's house by yourself?'

In spite of his seemingly genuine puzzlement, she refused to divulge her reasons. 'I simply wanted to do this on my own.'

'That may be, but your grandfather asked for my help. I won't quit in the middle of a project.' His jaw took on a familiar stubborn set which she knew from past experience warned her that he wouldn't budge his position. One thing was certain: she didn't have the power to fire him.

The more Rachel considered this new twist, the more she detected her grandmother's machinations. Hester hadn't wanted Rachel to walk away from a career she'd once loved, and now she would use Nick to convince her to return.

'Why did you accept his offer?' she asked, curious. 'If you can afford high-tech electronic gadgets, you can afford to rent an apartment or buy your own home.'

'Sorry to shatter your image, but I'm in debt to my eyebrows. It's a common result of spending all those years in medical school. I could have taken out a loan for a house, but for now all I need is this place. As for my electronic gadgets, as you call them, some people save their money for a fancy car. I saved mine for a stereo system.'

He clearly needed this project as much as she did, although for different reasons. 'So what are we going to do?' she asked.

'The only thing we *can* do,' he said. 'We work together. If we co-operate, we can whip this place into shape in no time.'

'If you say so.' Although she had her doubts, she also knew that the money her grandmother had inherited along with the house wouldn't last indefinitely. Rachel had learned long ago how to stretch a dollar until it squealed for mercy.

'Co-operation means that neither of us makes a decision—*any* decision—without the other's input,' she declared. 'You may have run the show when we were kids, but those days are over. Can you accept those terms?'

'Ah, Rachel's developed a backbone,' he said, his eyes shining with what she recognized as anticipation. 'I'm impressed.'

'I grew up,' she said shortly. 'About my terms…'

'I'm not sure you're in a position to be making any,' he said. At her splutter, he held up his hands. 'However, I agree to ask for your opinion before making any major decisions.'

She narrowed her eyes. 'What do you consider "major"?'

'Knocking out a wall, expanding the kitchen, adding a deck.'

'OK.' Marginally satisfied for the moment, Rachel moved toward the door. 'If you'll excuse me, I have to move my things and unpack.'

A doubtful expression appeared on his face. 'Why don't you stay here? There's plenty of room for the both of us. I'll take the sofa.'

She craved privacy so much she would have pitched a tent in the back yard. 'No, thanks.'

'There's no running water except on the first floor,' he warned. 'The plumber isn't coming for a few weeks yet.'

'Grams said he was coming on Monday.'

Nick shrugged. 'He called this morning and changed his plans. What can I say?'

'Then I'll drive across town like I'd originally planned.'

'For heaven's sake, Rachel,' he said, sounding exasperated. 'Don't be an idiot. You can use the shower here any time.'

Although she didn't want to see him more than necessary, it made more sense to walk across the yard than to go to her grandparents'. 'All right. Thanks. What about electricity?'

'The crew finished rewiring from top to bottom last week, so you can plug in your hair dryer and operate a microwave at the same time without blowing a fuse.'

'Then I'll be fine.'

'Suit yourself,' he said, surprising her by his calm acceptance of her decision. Nick never capitulated unless he was gearing to start the battle on a new front, which was why he had excelled in debate and had acted as captain of his squad.

'It's probably for the best, anyway,' he added easily. 'I come and go at crazy hours. I won't have to worry about disturbing you.'

'I thought you had all this free time to spend on the house?' A new thought came to her. 'Still the Romeo, I presume?'

'Jealous?' he teased.

She scoffed. Nick had always gone for beauty and not

brains. Since she hadn't fitted that category—and still didn't, in her opinion—she'd be foolish to waste the energy.

'Hardly. What you do on your own time is no concern of mine. Keep in mind, however, that I'm expecting you to do your fair share around here.'

'Don't worry about me,' he said cheerfully before he followed her down the steps. 'Want some help moving your things?'

'I can manage a couple of suitcases and a few boxes.'

Once again, and to her surprise, he acquiesced. 'If you change your mind, just give me a holler.'

An hour later, she'd moved her clothes into the cook's quarters off the north end of the kitchen. The room was medium-sized but, with a full-sized bed, a dresser and two nightstands, she only had a narrow path to walk in. The old house didn't have central air-conditioning and the small window unit in the living room didn't work, which meant that at six o'clock the inside temperature hadn't dropped in spite of the breeze coming through the window. A faint sheen of perspiration covered her skin by the time she'd unpacked, making her dream of a cool shower.

Unfortunately, Nick was home and she didn't want to knock on his door already.

After stashing her suitcases in the closet, she turned toward the kitchen for a cold drink. The sight of a man standing in the doorway sent her heart leaping into her throat. 'Don't do that!' she scolded Nick, waiting for her internal organs to settle back in place.

He grinned. 'Quit doing what? I was just standing here. It sure is hot, isn't it?'

'I know. That's why I'm going outside. Did you want something?'

'I'm requesting your presence for dinner.'

'Dinner?' She hadn't thought of food all afternoon. Then again, she hadn't had much of an appetite lately.

'Yeah, dinner. The meal after lunch and before breakfast.'

'I'm not hungry.'

'OK,' he said. 'Then you can watch me. I hate to eat alone.'

'I really don't—'

'If you don't want any of the fried chicken, at least have a sliver of French silk pie.'

French silk was her favorite, and her downfall.

'My place is also air-conditioned,' he added.

Rachel knew she'd probably live to regret it, but between chocolate dessert and cool temperatures she couldn't refuse. However, if the conversation strayed to more personal topics, she'd return to the heat. Physical discomfort was the least she could do to pay for her sins. 'All right.'

Deciding to take a shower while she was there, she grabbed a pair of black mesh athletic shorts and a matching Wichita State University vest.

While she nibbled on a drumstick and potato salad, Nick outlined the work he'd completed. 'Your grandparents and I cleaned out every room. We stored the best furniture in the east bedroom and got rid of the rest. Construction-wise, after I finish removing all the wallpaper, I intend to completely tear out the bad plasterboard until we're down to the studs. Then I want to go in and install the new sheet rock. After that, we'll be ready to paint or wallpaper, or do both.'

'So you're making this an assembly-line type of operation? Tear everything out and then go back and replace?'

He nodded. 'That's the easiest and most efficient way.'

Although Nick sounded matter-of-fact about his plans, she wouldn't have gone about this job in the same manner and she offered an alternative. 'I think it would be easier to tackle one room at a time, then the entire floor won't be unlivable.'

'But the rooms are empty and no one's living up there now,' he pointed out. 'So what difference does it make?'

None, she thought, except it was rather maddening to have her own ideas dismissed outright. Although she would have preferred more discussion, she also realized that she couldn't walk in and take over since he'd started the work. It didn't mean, however, that she had to like the situation.

He continued, apparently oblivious to her frustration. 'I'm hoping we'll have the second story done by the time the plumber finishes. Then we can finish the bathroom before we start on the main level.' He shoved the pie in front of her as he began clearing off the table. 'Have another piece.'

She pushed it back, noticing how Nick's single-mindedness hadn't changed. Neither had his propensity to steamroll his ideas through to completion.

'One slice is my limit,' she said politely as she rose to gather the dirty silverware.

'Go hop in the shower,' he told her. 'All I have to do is slide the pie back in the freezer, stuff the leftovers in the refrigerator and toss the dishes in the dishwasher. It'll only take a few minutes.'

'Thanks,' she said dryly, noting how he also still tended to organize people. For the most part, their friends had allowed him to do so, but Rachel had chafed under his directives. After running a household with her stepsister Marta after Marta's mother had died, Rachel had been too independent to follow Nick's commands without question. Inevitably, sparks had flown between them on a fairly regular basis. Rachel had never quite understood why they'd remained friends when they'd argued so often, but they had. It would be interesting to see if they were still on speaking terms by the time they'd finished the house.

'Towels are in the cupboard. Help yourself to whatever you might need.'

Rachel took Nick at his word. She felt strange, undressing in a room where Nick's aftershave permeated the air and his toiletries lined the basin, but she told herself to get used to it. Sharing a bathroom with Nick wouldn't be any different than sharing one with her grandparents.

Yeah, right, she scoffed. She wouldn't picture her grandpa shaving in front of the mirror while clad in only a pair of royal blue briefs. Neither would she borrow his shampoo and feel as if she were in his embrace.

Fifteen minutes later, she reappeared in Nick's living room. Her damp hair clung to her head in natural curls and she clutched her pile of clothes out of nervousness. Nick sat on the sofa with his feet propped on the coffee-table as he read a news magazine while Kenny G. provided the background music.

'Feeling better?' he asked.

'Much.' Suddenly ill-at-ease, she edged toward the door. 'I should go.'

'Did you plan something for this evening?'

'No...'

'If neither of us are doing anything special, we may as well do it together.'

She sat down on the ancient recliner, not as eager to leave the cool comfort of his apartment as she'd thought.

He closed the magazine and located the TV program guide. 'How about television?'

'I'd rather listen to music. He's wonderful, isn't he?' she asked, referring to Kenny G.

'I think so, too.'

Falling silent, she listened to the melody and let the notes wash over her. When the CD ended, she sighed.

'Tired?' he asked.

'A little. It's been a long day.'

'I noticed you're wearing a WSU T-shirt,' he began. 'Did you earn your nursing degree there?'

Her relaxed mood disappeared and tension now filled her. She sat up, her spine stiff. 'Whatever are you talking about?'

CHAPTER THREE

NICK held up his hands, more than ready to call her bluff in order to have his questions answered. 'Come on, Rachel. I saw you in action, remember?'

Her tension slowly eased, although her eyes still held a wary look. He would have to tread carefully on this apparently sore subject.

'I graduated seven years ago,' she said.

'Did you work in Wichita since then, or did you move on?'

'I stayed.'

'There are a lot of good hospitals there. After med school, I did my internship and residence at St Luke's.'

She didn't comment and he pressed on. 'Where did you work?'

'Via Christi. St Joseph campus.'

Her clipped comment told him that she was still close-mouthed when she wanted to be. Getting information out of her when she wasn't inclined to share was like pulling a stubborn tooth. From the way she clenched her hands together, he was surprised she hadn't run from the room. Maybe she realized that it wouldn't do any good: he knew where she lived.

'I liked family practice the best,' he commented, hoping to put her at ease with stories of his own past. 'I thought about internal medicine, but internists don't deliver babies.'

'You don't now, do you?'

'Only because the hospital is too small to afford the liability,' he said. 'However, I've welcomed a few wee ones into the world when their moms couldn't make the thirty-mile drive to Joplin. What was your favorite area?'

There was a brief pause. 'You're not going to let this drop, are you?'

He grinned. 'What do you think?'

She hesitated before a deep sigh signaled her defeat. Yet he felt sure that, although she was opening up, she wouldn't totally unburden herself. Regardless, winning the little battles would eventually win the war.

'ER,' she said. 'I worked in ER.'

Nick leaned back, careful to present himself at ease so as not to put her back on the defensive. 'What brings you to this neck of the woods?'

'I told you before,' she said avoiding his gaze. 'I'm helping my grandparents. Why did *you* come back?'

'Hooper is on the list of under-served areas for physicians and coming here has paid off some of the debt I owe, but that was only partly the reason for my return. I came back because of my dad.'

'Your father? I thought he died when you were young.'

'He committed suicide when I was three. Apparently he suffered severe post-traumatic stress from his days in 'Nam and had more bad days than good.'

'Oh, Nick. All those years of being around you and I didn't know the circumstances,' she said, her eyes filled with sympathy.

'Ancient history. Anyway, when I was about six, some kids hassled me about how I'd end up like my dad—a good-for-nothing mental case. I ran home that day, crying, and my mom told me how he'd been a straight-A student and a popular kid in school. When he came home from his tour of duty, he wanted to forget everything and step back into his old life, but he couldn't. His memories wouldn't let him.'

He paused, remembering the incident as if it had happened yesterday. His mother had pulled him close, showed him high-school photos and mementos and told him of his father's dreams for his only son. 'She told me to do my best and I'd make my dad proud.'

'So you spent your whole life being an over-achiever.'

He shrugged. 'More or less.'

'You were certainly successful. Everyone thought highly of you. They still do.'

He grinned. 'Music to my ears.'

'Don't let it go to your head. Are you going to stay here when your time is up, or move on?'

'I'll probably stick around,' he said. 'I'm a small-town guy at heart.'

'What about your mom and your sisters? Where are they?'

'My sisters are scattered all over Missouri and my mom moved to Springfield. We're close enough to keep tabs on each other, but far enough apart to stay out of each other's hip pocket.'

'I'm glad your life has worked out the way you wanted it,' she said softly. 'That isn't always the case.'

'What about your family?' he asked.

'Marta is in Dallas with her husband, Evan. She and Amy are both nurse-practitioners. Amy, by the way, is planning a December wedding in Maple Corners.' Her expression softened as she apparently pictured her siblings. 'Evan and Amy's fiancé, Ryan, are doctors, so whenever we get together it makes for interesting dinner conversation.'

'Sounds like medicine runs in the Wyman sisters' blood.'

Her smile wavered. 'I guess it does.'

'Since Marta and Amy are attached, are you the odd man out when the Wyman clan visits?'

'If you're asking if I have a special someone in my life, then the answer is yes. Charles is in charge of the hospital information system.'

'Is he coming to Hooper soon?' Nick asked, curious about the fellow Rachel had chosen. 'I'd like to meet him.'

'We haven't made any specific plans, but when he does, I'll introduce you.'

'That would be great.' Keeping his tone offhanded, he seized the opportunity to discuss her profession. 'We really could use a nurse of your caliber at Hooper General.'

'No.' Her voice was abrupt before she took a deep breath. 'I don't have time to work in health care.'

'Maybe not full time, but part—'

'No.'

'If you're on a leave of absence, I'm sure we could work something out.'

'I'm not. I quit.'

He leaned forward. 'What happened, Rachel?' he asked softly.

Rachel squared her shoulders. 'I don't want to talk about it.'

He couldn't drop the subject, not when he sensed that a breakthrough lay within his grasp. 'Something drove you away from your career and your home.'

'I needed a change, that's all. Must you read more into the situation than necessary?' She jumped to her feet and began to pace. 'Lots of people change jobs. In fact, statistics show that most people will have three careers in their lifetime. I'm in transition. Please, Nick, let it rest.'

Her petition, uttered in what he considered near-desperation, made it impossible for him to continue. He consoled himself with the idea of other opportunities. 'If you say so.'

'I do.' She headed toward the door. 'It's getting late and I've had a long day. Thanks for dinner. I'll cook next time.'

'Tomorrow?' he asked hopefully.

Her smile seemed weak. 'Only if you promise not to hound me about working at the hospital.'

He faked a frown. 'You drive a hard bargain, Ms Wyman, but it's a deal. Come on. I'll walk you home.'

'That isn't necessary,' she protested. 'I'm only going across the yard.'

'Humor me,' he said, and he followed her down the stairs and into the yard shaded by a variety of deciduous trees. The wind rustled the leaves in a soft whisper as Nick accompanied her to the west side of the house, where a large commercial dumpster stood conveniently underneath the upstairs balcony and outside the back door, clearly ready for the debris from their renovation project.

'Is the old story of Great-Aunt Matilda's buried treasure still making the rounds among the kids?' Rachel asked.

Nick laughed. 'It's not just the kids who are fixated on that old myth. Adults have asked me if I've found any chests of gold or silver hidden in the walls of the Boyd mansion. They were teasing, of course, but who doesn't like the prospect of finding legendary riches?'

She shook her head. 'I wonder how the rumor got started.'

'Someone took a story and over time romanticized it. Matilda being a recluse only added to the mystery. Considering the property has stood empty for the last year, I'm surprised someone didn't sneak in and tear up the place.'

'It's almost a shame they didn't.'

Nick fell into step beside her as they walked across the yard. 'Good grief, woman! Don't we have enough work to do?'

She chuckled. 'If they'd torn out the walls for us, we'd be ahead of schedule.'

'I see your point.' Nick stopped at the back door, opened it, then flicked on the light switch before allowing her past. 'Be sure and lock the doors.'

She rolled her eyes. 'I will, but Hooper isn't exactly a hotbed of criminal activity.'

'We have our share,' he said. 'The kids who show up in ER spaced out on drugs are getting them from someone. They're not afraid to steal anything that isn't bolted down if it will provide the money to buy their fixes.'

'I'd hoped the drug culture had bypassed Hooper.'

'Not in this day and age of the Internet.'

She shook her head. 'Makes our teepee-ing houses and smashing pumpkins in the streets on Hallowe'en seem tame.'

'Yeah. It makes sense to be cautious, no matter where you live.'

'How true.' She hesitated. 'Thanks again for the dinner.'

'You're welcome.'

He caught himself leaning forward to kiss her, then stopped himself. He'd stolen several kisses from her over the years—if his feeble attempts could be called that—but sneaking one at his age didn't hold the same allure and definitely wouldn't hold the same satisfaction. He wanted her to be a willing participant, and at this point in the game she wouldn't be.

'Goodnight, Nick.'

''Night.' Turning on one heel, he heard the quiet snick of the lock, then a louder clank as Rachel shot the deadbolt home. He wondered what she'd say if he told her the real reason why she should lock her doors.

To protect herself from him.

'I can't believe you didn't tell me about Nick,' Rachel told her grandparents the next afternoon.

'We probably should have,' Hester answered, casting a frown upon her husband of fifty-two years, 'but your grandfather started organizing everything without telling me...'

Wilbur shook his gray head. He was a tall man who towered head and shoulders over his petite wife. Between his hobbies and spending time with his cronies, he was still spry for his age.

'If you'll recall, Hester, you asked me to find someone to work on the house, which I did. The next thing I knew, you'd asked Rachel to help, too.' He reached across the table and patted her hand. 'Don't get me wrong. We're as happy as bees in clover to have you here, honey. With you and Nick working together, you'll get done in half the time.'

'Thanks, Gramps, but—'

'Anyway,' Hester interrupted, 'after we'd realized what we'd done, we were afraid you wouldn't come if you knew about our deal with Nick.'

'So we agreed to keep quiet and let the chips fall where they may,' Wilbur finished.

'It still would have been nice to know what sort of situation I was walking into,' Rachel argued.

'That's just it, dear,' Hester said. 'You and Nick were horribly competitive as children and with your…problems I was afraid you wouldn't come if you knew you'd see him on a regular basis.'

Wilbur joined in. 'You were adamant about steering clear of anything related to medicine. Hester thought it might be the last straw for you to be around Nick and you'd go to the Alaskan wilderness or some such place.'

'Be honest, Rachel,' Hester began. 'Would you have come to Hooper, even for a few weeks, if you'd known of our arrangement with Nick?'

'No,' Rachel answered honestly.

'See!' Hester shot her husband a triumphant glance before she turned a gaze filled with sympathy on Rachel. 'I always regretted that we lived so far away from you girls as you were growing up. I wanted to be closer than a phone call when one of you three had a problem, but I couldn't. I literally *lived* for those summers when you and Marta and Amy were mine to spoil.'

'The same goes for me, honey,' Wilbur added.

Tears burned at the back of Rachel's eyes. She'd known how delighted her grandparents had been to open their home for June, July and most of August. She simply hadn't realized how much.

Hester coughed politely and blinked rapidly. 'So once we realized how you were suffering, I wanted you to be here with us while you sorted things out.'

Rachel rose and hugged her grandparents in turn. 'I'm glad I came.'

Her grandfather smiled. 'Even though we kept a few secrets from you?'

She returned his grin with a wide one of her own. 'Even then.'

'Good,' Wilbur said. 'Now Hester can stop worrying about you two and start sleeping again at night.'

'We're adults, Grams. We don't fight any more.' Actually, her thoughts ran in a far different direction. She wouldn't mind freely sharing a kiss with Nick—*a real* one, not one of those quick little pecks he'd given her from time to time to tease her.

'Where *is* he?' Hester asked. 'I didn't see his car when we drove up.'

'I don't know,' Rachel answered. 'I heard him leave about an hour ago.'

'Maybe he was invited out to lunch,' Wilbur said. 'With all the meal invitations he's received, the boy doesn't need to cook if he doesn't want to.'

'Really?' The news wasn't surprising, but a familiar sense of disgruntlement swept over her. Nick, the ladies' man, was alive and well...and clearly out of reach. 'He invited me over to share his take-out chicken dinner last night.'

'How sweet of him,' Hester gushed. 'He's a real gem, Rachel. You should set your cap at him.'

Rachel retrieved another handful of ice cubes from the freezer and dropped them into her glass. 'He's out of my league, Grams,' she said lightly, although she wished it were otherwise.

'Don't be ridiculous.'

'One thing's for sure,' Wilbur said. 'There will be a lot of disappointed women in town when he gets hitched. Oh, to have that much energy, hey, Hester?' He winked at her.

Hester rose and playfully swatted him. 'Oh, you. Now, go on and visit Jack while Rachel and I visit.'

Rachel breathed easier as Wilbur scooted his chair away from the table and carried his cup of coffee to the sink. The subject was closed and, hopefully, would stay that way.

'How long will your hen party last?' he asked.

'At least an hour, maybe longer,' Hester declared.

'Good. We'll have time for a few hands of gin, then.'

'Leave him a few matchsticks, will you? And don't forget the gingerbread.' Hester turned to Rachel as soon as Wilbur started for the front door, whistling a jaunty tune. 'Have you met Jack Rexton yet?'

'I haven't met any of the neighbors,' Rachel confessed. 'Only Nick, and he really doesn't count.'

'Jack and your grandfather have been friends for ages. His wife died several years ago and, with his health problems, he doesn't get out much. Wilbur usually checks on him every few days and I always send goodies for him.' She leaned closer and winked. 'Don't tell your grandpa, but I've been making sure Nick's sweet tooth doesn't bother him. He loves my gingerbread, you know.'

Rachel laughed. 'Who doesn't? Are you going to share with me, too?'

'Of course, dear, but didn't I give you the recipe?'

'Mine doesn't taste the same. Yours is so much better.'

'Pshaw,' Hester said, her eyes shimmering with pleasure over Rachel's compliment. 'Just keep trying. Oh, before I forget, I told Nick he could use the washer and dryer. So if you find a strange pile of clothes, you'll know why.'

Immediately, Rachel pictured a laundry basket filled with Nick's unmentionables in a bold array of colors. It was enough to make her heart race.

'Anything else I should know about?' she asked dryly.

'I don't think so. Now,' Hester said briskly, 'let's go upstairs and you can tell me your plans. By the way, I do hope you can fix the squeaky boards in the hallway. They've creaked for as long as I can remember. Matilda always complained about the noise but, as far as I know, no one ever bothered to fix them.'

'I'll add squeaky floorboards to our list,' Rachel promised.

Rachel and her grandmother spent the next twenty minutes discussing the merits of stenciled designs versus wallpaper. Before they'd finished, the telephone on the table outside the master bedroom rang.

'I wonder who it is,' Rachel said, hoping it might be Nick as she raised the receiver.

It wasn't.

'Rachel, you must come over here right away,' Wilbur said without preamble.

'What's wrong?'

'Jack. He can't breathe.'

Rachel asked what she considered the obvious. 'Did you call an ambulance?'

'The stubborn fool won't let me. Says it will pass, but it hasn't. He's been like this for ten minutes and I'm getting worried.'

'What's going on?' Hester whispered.

'It's Grandpa. He says Jack can't breathe.'

'Oh, dear.'

Rachel might have accused her grandparents of orchestrating these events, but the worry on her grandmother's face wasn't feigned. If she was concerned about Jack, then she obviously had good reason.

She spoke into the receiver. 'I'll be there in two shakes.'

'I wonder if his emphysema is worse,' Hester remarked as she followed Rachel downstairs.

'I won't know until I get there.'

Rachel dodged the worst of the rickety front porch steps and took off in the direction Hester had indicated, while her grandmother followed at a slower pace. The Rexton home was a two story brownstone that stood directly across the street and was in marginally better condition than Great-Aunt Matilda's.

Wilbur must have been watching for her because he opened the door before she started up the steps.

'He's not any better,' he said. 'He's been on oxygen the whole time, but I can't see it making a difference.'

'Any luck on talking him into an ambulance ride?'

Wilbur shook his head as he stepped aside to allow her entrance. 'Stubborn is what he is.'

'Maybe I can convince him.'

Wilbur escorted her to the living room where he'd left his friend. His introduction was hearty and his voice lacked the worry Rachel had heard earlier. 'Jack, this is my granddaughter, Rachel. She's trying to get Matilda's house ready to sell, so you'll be seeing her a lot in the next few weeks. Did I mention she's a nurse, like my other granddaughters?'

Jack Rexton, an average-built man in his seventies with a ring of gray hair around his balding pate, sat on the sofa. He was connected to the portable oxygen tank between his legs by a length of tubing and his nasal cannula. Perspiration dotted his brow and upper lip.

He acknowledged her presence by slightly raising one hand off his knee. 'Pleased…to…meet…you.'

Rachel moved into the chair next to the end of the sofa where Jack sat. 'Gramps called me because he's concerned about you. He figures if you can't play gin, you must be sick.'

A faint smile crossed Jack's lined features and a gaze reflecting his fondness for his old buddy drifted toward Wilbur and Hester, who'd finally joined them. 'Worry… wort.'

'I can see you're having trouble,' Rachel said, hearing the wheezes and crackles in his lungs with every shallow breath and noticing the blue tinge to his nail beds. 'Would you mind if I gave you a little check-up? I give them free of charge to my neighbors.' She grinned.

'Go…ahead. Wasting…your…time…though. Better…in a…few…'

Rachel didn't squander a moment. She immediately took his pulse, then counted his respirations, aware that more than thirty-five per minute could mean he would need mechanical ventilation. He was at thirty, which was pushing his luck.

'Have you been sick within the last few days?'

'A…cold.'

'I'm going to unbutton your shirt so I can watch you breathe.' Within moments, she had his chest bared. He had the traditional barrel-shaped chest common in emphysema sufferers, and the spaces between his ribs seemed more pronounced as the intercostal muscles had clearly retracted in order to help ventilation.

There was no question in Rachel's mind. Jack needed a hospital and he needed its services now.

'You have to see a doctor,' she said gently but firmly. 'I

suspect you've developed pneumonia. You need antibiotics and fluids, and respiratory therapy.'

'No…ambulance.'

'Why not?' she asked. 'They'll have medicines ready to give you…'

He shook his head and his face appeared flushed as he tried to be vehement in his refusal. 'No… Wife…died…in…one.'

Rachel understood completely. Walking into an emergency room posed the same problem for her.

'Now, Jack,' Hester interrupted. 'Eloise had a massive heart attack. It could have happened anywhere.'

Jack's mouth formed a hard line and he gave a brisk chop with his hand.

Rachel turned to Wilbur. 'Check and see if Nick is back.'

'Jack's bad, isn't he?' Wilbur asked in a tone meant only for her ears.

'I'm afraid he might be in respiratory failure,' Rachel admitted. 'He can't stay at home. Maybe Nick will convince him to go.'

Wilbur went to the door to check and returned, shaking his head. She crouched in front of Jack and offered the next option. 'All right, no ambulance.' At Hester's gasp, she continued, 'But will you go to the hospital if we take you?'

Jack nodded.

'I'll have Grandpa bring his car around.'

Wilbur didn't wait for further instructions. He disappeared and seconds later the front door slammed to indicate where he'd gone.

'I'll pack a few things for him,' Hester said, before she headed upstairs, presumably in search of Jack's bedroom. By the time she returned with a small overnight bag, Rachel had gathered the many vials of prescription medication, ranging from drugs to lower Jack's blood pressure and cholesterol, to hypothyroidism, to controlling heart arrhythmia. Her grandmother's comment about Jack having health problems was clearly accurate.

By the time she'd filled a bag with all of his pills, Wilbur had re-entered through the kitchen door.

'I pulled into the driveway, next to the back door,' he said. 'He won't have as far to walk.'

Rachel shuffled the older man to the car in his slippers, grateful for her grandfather's assistance. In spite of Jack's frail appearance, he was still more than she could handle on her own.

Within ten minutes, Wilbur pulled into the hospital's drive. 'Go to the emergency entrance,' Rachel directed. 'I'll run in and ask for a wheelchair.'

Bracing herself for what she might find inside, she rushed in and was relieved to discover the department was quiet. Unlike the ER she'd worked in, Hooper General's emergency room was arranged like a wheel, with the nurses' station forming the center while the exam rooms branched off in every direction for maximum visibility. Two were labeled TRAUMA and were enclosed in glass with curtains for privacy. Others were regular rooms, complete with solid doors that now stood ajar.

Rachel strode toward a woman wearing maternity scrubs who carried an armload of IV sets as she rounded the desk.

'I have a man outside in respiratory distress,' Rachel announced, before she recited more details in short, crisp language.

Merrilee, according to her name badge, was an RN, and she moved fast in spite of her ungainly shape. She called for Darrel, an LPN, who came out of another empty room at a fast clip.

Between the three of them, they wheeled Jack into a large exam room. Merrilee placed the oximeter on Jack's finger to determine his oxygen saturation, and in seconds Rachel saw the low number on the digital display. As soon as the nurse had taken a brief history, the ER physician walked in.

'How long have you been like this?' Dr Gower asked Jack after he'd listened to his patient's chest.

Jack held up one finger.

He turned to Merrilee and barked out his orders. 'Blood gas, stat. I want a chest X-ray, along with a CBC, electro-lytes, urinalysis, blood and sputum cultures.'

'Yes, sir.' The young woman who was eight months preg-nant in Rachel's estimation, waddled away, obviously intent on notifying the lab, Radiology and Respiratory Therapy. Undoubtedly, she would also contact Medical Records for copies of any previous treatment or admissions.

Dr Gower addressed Rachel. 'Are you related to him?'

She shook her head. 'Neighbors.'

'Jack's a good friend and I check on him every few days,' Wilbur added. 'When I saw he wasn't doing too well today, I called my granddaughter to look at him. She's a nurse and I thought she could convince him to see a doctor.'

Rachel wanted to clap her hand over her grandfather's mouth. Did he have to tell everyone about her? she thought crossly, feeling, then seeing the doctor's speculative gaze turn on her.

'He's lucky you did,' Dr Gower commented. 'As ill as he is, he'll be here for a while. His lungs are full of fluid and he's flirting with respiratory failure.'

'I suspected as much,' Rachel said.

'If you'd like to sit in the lobby, we'll call you when he's back from Radiology.'

'All right.' Rachel ushered her grandparents through the ER's double doors to the chairs closest to the emergency department.

'How long will it take?' Hester asked.

Rachel found a three-month-old magazine—the newest in the pile—and thumbed through the dog-eared pages. 'About thirty to forty-five minutes,' she predicted. If her grandfather hadn't needed her for moral support, she would have asked him to drive her home. Sitting in the sterile atmosphere of a hospital wasn't her idea of a relaxing Sunday afternoon.

'Do you think he'll make it?' Wilbur asked.

'Cases like his are unpredictable,' she said, unwilling to

commit herself to a prognosis. 'He seems like a tough old bird, though.'

'He is at that,' Hester declared. 'He told me that he had to learn how to do his own laundry after Eloise passed on. I don't mind telling you he wore the strangest colored clothes for a long time. Until I wrote out a list of what temperature settings to use.' She smiled.

'Jack doesn't belong at home by himself,' Wilbur said after a short pause. 'He needs someone to look after him.'

'It probably would be for the best,' Rachel agreed.

'He'd hate being in a nursing home,' Hester said. 'But I suppose there are times when we really have no choice.'

At the moment, Rachel could relate to the frustrating feeling most strongly. She would like nothing better than to have the doctor report Jack's miraculous recovery so they could return home, but she knew it wasn't possible. She was destined for a long wait. Luckily, the ER was quiet and she hoped it would stay that way as long as she was this close to the department.

Deep in her thoughts, it surprised her when someone slid into the seat beside her—someone wearing a familiar masculine scent.

Nick's wide grin made him appear more like a boy than a skilled physician, in spite of his monogrammed white coat. He leaned closer to speak in her ear. 'For a woman who doesn't want anything to do with medicine, isn't it ironic how often our professional paths cross?'

CHAPTER FOUR

'DON'T I know it,' Rachel said fervently. 'What are you doing here?'

'Making rounds.' Nick glanced at Wilbur and Hester. 'What about you?'

'Jack Rexton was having trouble breathing,' Wilbur offered. 'He wouldn't let me call an ambulance, but Rachel talked him into coming to the hospital if we drove him. So here we are.'

'How's he doing?' Nick asked.

'We're waiting for his test results,' Rachel said.

Nick straightened. 'I'll see how they're coming.' He paused. 'Want to come along, Rachel?'

She refused to walk back into an area that reminded her so vividly of her failures. 'I'll stay here.'

His expression became inscrutable, but he didn't argue. 'Suit yourself.'

Dr Gower came out about ten minutes later. 'We're moving Mr Rexton to Intensive Care until we can stabilize his oxygen levels. He has pneumonia and is also dehydrated, so we've started him on IV antibiotics and fluids, along with medication to break up the mucus in his lungs.'

'His prognosis?' Rachel asked.

'He's a very sick man,' the doctor explained. 'The pH of his blood is near critical levels and his carbon dioxide level is high. There's a real chance we'll have to rely on mechanical ventilation, which is why I want him in ICU where he'll be closely monitored. He could rally quickly, but then again, considering his age and general health...' His voice faded as he shrugged.

'Can we see him, Doctor?' Hester asked.

'You can ride along in the elevator, but visiting times on the unit are extremely limited. You're only allowed ten minutes every other hour. We should also notify his next of kin.'

'His daughter lives in New Orleans,' Hester answered. 'Jack probably has her phone number in his billfold.'

'I'll ask. The admissions clerk needs the information to process his paperwork. Do you know if he has a living will or any advance directives?'

Rachel was quite familiar with the forms he'd mentioned. They gave the medical staff notice of an individual's wishes in terms of resuscitation orders and other life-sustaining measures.

Wilbur nodded. 'He's got both. You probably have them on file from his last hospital stay.'

'We'll look into it.' Dr Gower held the doors for them to pass through. Hester and Wilbur went ahead, but Rachel held her ground.

'Why don't you two go with Jack?' she suggested. 'I'll wait here.' At Hester's frown, she added, 'Out of the way.'

'What if Jack needs you?' Hester addressed the doctor. 'If it weren't for my granddaughter talking Jack into coming, he wouldn't be here at all. She's here to work on our house with Nick, but she's really a nurse, you know.'

Rachel heard the pride in her grandmother's voice, saw the look of interest flash in Dr Gower's eyes again and wanted to shrink out of sight. Her dear grandparents, whether by design or accident, had effectively overridden her wish to maintain a low profile. She wondered now if she'd find her name and credentials listed on the 'What's New' page in the Hooper newspaper.

'I believe your husband mentioned it earlier,' Dr Gower said, then addressed Rachel. 'I'd be happy to give you a guided tour of our newly remodeled ER.' He grinned. 'We just took down our ''Wet Paint'' signs a few weeks ago.'

'I don't want to interrupt your busy schedule,' she began.

'It's quiet for now,' he said cheerfully. 'There's plenty of space for everyone.'

With three pairs of eyes trained on her, Rachel had no choice but to concede. She followed her grandparents, aware of Dr Gower falling into step behind her. A chuckle caught her attention and she saw Nick deep in conversation with an admissions clerk—a girl who couldn't have been more than twenty. From Nick's laughter and her giggles, Rachel doubted the two were discussing hospital business.

Nick glanced in Rachel's direction at the same moment and she raised one eyebrow. *Ever the flirt*, she mentally challenged.

He'd obviously read her thoughts because he shrugged helplessly. Rachel shook her head. Nick would never change, she decided.

Within seconds of her conclusion, Merrilee and Darrel pushed Jack's bed out of his cubicle.

'Why don't you let Nick and this nice doctor show you around while we see that Jack gets settled?' Hester asked.

'But—'

'We'll only be a few minutes,' Wilbur told her, before they hurried after their old friend.

Before she could refuse Dr Gower's previous offer of a guided tour, Nick motioned her toward the desk, where the ER physician had joined him.

'Dylan, I'd like to introduce you to an old friend, Rachel Wyman.'

Dylan stuck out his hand, his bland professional expression now transformed into a bright smile that reminded her of Nick's. Some would also claim the other physician was equally as handsome, but Rachel disagreed. She'd always been drawn to dark-haired men, not blonds.

'You're the woman at the hardware store,' he said, as if he'd just realized her identity. 'Nick's told me about you.'

Rachel shot Nick a glare, not fooled by his innocent who-me? expression. 'Oh, he did, did he?'

'Don't worry. Everything he said was good,' Dylan assured her. 'Speaking of good, Nick, how was lunch with Andrea?'

'The meal was awful,' Nick answered. 'If they're serving baked chicken or fish for tonight's entrée, choose a chef's salad. How hospital cooks can make all food tasteless is beyond me.'

Rachel immediately homed in on the woman's name although Nick apparently didn't consider her company as important. Regardless, her grandfather had been correct. Nick, even while on duty, had had time for a luncheon date with his latest conquest.

Dylan shrugged. 'It's a gift, I'm sure.' He winked at Rachel and she returned his smile. 'Ready for the tour?'

'Actually—' she began.

'Of course she is,' Nick interrupted. 'How could she possibly pass up an opportunity to see the hospital's latest pride and joy?'

With both men's gazes locked on her, Rachel could hardly refuse. 'All right, but I don't want to take you away from your other duties.'

Nick skirted the desk to accompany them. 'Don't be ridiculous. I'm waiting for a lab report and Dylan normally spends Sunday afternoons with his feet up.'

'Says you,' Dylan answered without rancor. Clearly, the two men were good friends and each gave as good as he got. Yet, for all their teasing, she suspected that both men would display their crisp, professional personas when necessary.

As the two men guided her through what seemed like every inch of their facility, she felt like the *crème* filling of an Oreo cookie. It wasn't unpleasant, being sandwiched between two handsome men, especially when one of them was Nick, but her latent fear of the ambulance bay doors whooshing open with a trauma patient kept her from truly enjoying the experience.

Finally, they had gone full circle and stood in front of

the nurse's desk once again. 'Thanks for the tour,' she said politely.

'My pleasure,' Dylan said. 'If you get bored with holding a paintbrush, come back. Merrilee is going on maternity leave soon and so far we don't have anyone to replace her.'

'I'm sure you'll find someone,' Rachel replied, careful not to volunteer or to act as if she would consider doing so.

'Just think about it,' Dylan pressed.

She glared at Nick, certain he'd planted the idea in Dylan's head, but Nick's hooded gaze and noncommittal expression suggested his innocence. She sensed his interest in her reply, but the two-way radio on the counter behind the desk prevented her from giving one.

'Hooper Gen.,' came the deep, disembodied voice through static-filled air. 'This is squad two-eleven.'

Anxiety and fear spread through Rachel as it had ever since the fateful night she'd worked in ER and dealt with another ambulance crew's emergency. She'd never wanted to head for the lobby as badly as she did at this moment, but her feet simply wouldn't move. Instead, she tried to block her ears from hearing the details, but couldn't.

Dylan immediately pressed a button. 'This is Hooper Gen. Go ahead, two-eleven.'

'We have a thirty-five-year-old female with possible neck injuries from an auto accident. Vitals are stable, but she's complaining of pain.'

'Any other injuries?'

'A scrape on her forehead from the air bag. The other driver isn't reporting any problems. ETA is ten minutes.'

'Ten-four.'

Rachel slowly released the breath she'd been holding. It was probably a case of whiplash. Serious enough to the victim, but relatively minor in comparison to broken bones and internal injuries.

'Hooper Gen.?' came the voice again.

'Go ahead,' Dylan replied.

'We have a male, forty-two years of age, with a possible broken ankle. Stand by for vitals.' The EMT's observations came a few minutes later. 'BP is one-seventy over one hundred. Pulse is eighty-five.'

'Stabilize and transport,' Dylan replied.

'Sounds like you're going to be busy in a few minutes,' Nick said. 'Want me to stick around?'

'For a neck and an ankle?' Dylan chortled. 'I can handle those in my sleep with one hand tied behind my back.'

Rachel swallowed hard and wiped away the droplets of perspiration that had suddenly formed on her forehead. Her stomach twisted until she thought she might lose her lunch. She simply couldn't stand here, even if she wasn't being called upon to perform nursing duties.

Without casting a second glance in Nick's direction, she headed for the exit. Even the lobby seemed too close to potential tragedy for her comfort.

'If my grandparents show up, tell them I'm waiting in the car,' she said, hating to hear her voice tremble.

'Why don't you wait here?' Nick asked as she inched toward the same entrance she'd used earlier. 'There's an extra chair. You can sit back and observe.'

Dylan seconded his opinion. 'You won't be in the way.'

She shook her head. 'No, I can't. I need…' Her throat closed off the words 'to get away' and she substituted 'fresh air' before she broke into a near run.

Halfway to her escape, Nick caught up to her. 'Wait in the lobby. It's hotter than Hades outside.'

How could she explain that by staying, even in the lobby, she'd entered her own private hell? She shook her arm free of his grip. 'My grandparents will be along shortly. Just tell them where I am!'

She rushed to the doors leading to the parking lot, squeezing through before they'd fully opened. Several minutes and many calming breaths later, she realized that she had no idea where her grandfather had parked his Oldsmobile. No matter. She knew it on sight and would rather walk the rows in the blistering heat then go back inside.

The ambulance came from the west and slowly pulled into the emergency entrance's driveway. She turned her back on a scene she knew by heart but her actions couldn't block out the sound of voices carrying on the breeze—the tell-tale snap of the gurney wheels locking into place, the cargo doors slamming shut or the hospital's electric doors whooshing open.

Rachel walked the pavement in search of the familiar older model tan vehicle. The sun's rays beat down on her head but, in spite of the heat, her arms were cold and she rubbed at the goose bumps that had appeared. It shouldn't be long until her grandparents returned, provided Nick passed along her message.

She gritted her teeth, knowing how her grandparents would worry about her once they learned of her abrupt exit. She could already picture the concern on their faces but she was certain they wouldn't press her for details.

Nick, however, was another story.

He would demand an explanation for why she'd torn herself out of his grasp and run like a frightened cottontail. But she wasn't about to go into detail about what she'd done—or, more appropriately, what she *hadn't* done. Some people could talk about whatever bothered them, but talking wouldn't undo the past. If unloading her guilt on the hospital chaplain hadn't eased her conscience, she saw no point in rehashing the subject with Nick.

If only she'd refused her grandmother's gentle manipulation to stay behind while they escorted Jack to his room. She'd never been able to say no very well, least of all to her grandparents. Clearly, Hester had taken advantage of her weakness.

She spied her grandfather's car just as she saw them approach out of the corner of her eye. The concern on her grandmother's face matched the expression Rachel had expected to see, and she braced herself for another conversation on what she considered a forbidden subject.

Hester's smile seemed forced. 'I'm sorry we took so long, dear,' she said, sounding tired. 'We tried to hurry, but we had a terrible time getting an elevator.'

The extra lines of stress on Hester's face concerned Rachel, although she knew her grandmother wouldn't appreciate her granddaughter fussing over her. 'No problem,' she said lightly, pretending all was right with the world. 'I was getting chilly inside so I asked Nick to tell you where I was. They must have the air-conditioning thermostat set to below freezing. Did you notice how all the staff wore sweaters and long sleeves?'

Wilbur nodded as he unlocked the car doors. 'I was getting cold myself. Are you girls ready to go? I don't know about you two, but my old ticker has had enough excitement for one day.'

Rachel released the breath she'd been holding. Obviously Nick hadn't said a word about her flighty actions in ER. Her grandparents' preoccupation was obviously due to their worry over Jack and not her.

The atmosphere during the ride home was rather subdued and Rachel tried to lift the older couple's spirits. 'I'm sure Jack is in good hands,' she commented. 'Dr Gower seemed to know what he was doing.'

'I'm sure he does,' Hester said. 'It's just hard to see another of our friends suffer from a serious illness. When you get to our age and are in the middle of your autumn years, you can't look too far into the future.'

'I'm not so sure that *any* of us can,' Rachel said, remembering the young people she'd seen in the ER who'd gone to the morgue instead of home to their families. 'No one knows what tomorrow, or even the next hour, will bring.'

Hester sighed. 'So true.'

Trying to dispel the maudlin mood, Rachel teased, 'On the other hand, with today's medical technology, you both could live another thirty years. Just think of the party that

Marta, Amy and I will throw for you to celebrate your hundredth birthdays! You'll probably get a card from the President and be interviewed on *Good Morning, America*.'

Hester giggled. 'You're so right, dear. We must live each moment to the full, and not get bogged down in what we can't change.'

Wilbur stopped in front of the house. 'I promised to look after Jack's place while he's gone,' he said. 'If you see anything unusual, will you call us?'

'I'll keep my eyes open,' Rachel promised as she slid out of the back seat and slammed the car door.

'We'll swing by to pick up his mail and the newspaper,' Hester said. 'So don't worry about that.'

Rachel lifted her hand in farewell and watched the two drive down the street, relieved that the need for pretense was over. She may have fooled her grandparents, but she still had to face her worst critic. Rather than test her acting abilities, she intended to steer clear of Nick by burying herself in work.

Nick ambled toward the main house from the direction of his garage apartment with his bag of laundry slung over one shoulder and a jug of raspberry lemonade in his hand. He took his time, not because he wasn't in a hurry but because approaching slowly gave him time to review his game plan. It was as plain as the lumber stacked along the south side of the house that Rachel wouldn't be happy to see him. Luckily, he had his own key, so if she thought a locked door would keep him out, it wouldn't.

Reading her thoughts came easily to him, partly because he'd known her so well, partly because her character hadn't changed over the years and partly because her beautiful face reflected her emotions like a well-polished mirror.

Because he faced challenges head on, Rachel would expect him to charge in and demand an answer as to why she'd run out of the ER faster than most people responded to a code blue. And because she expected him to ask questions, she would do her best to maintain her distance, which also meant that the dinner she'd promised him had probably become a thing of the past.

Standing outside the back door, he paused from knocking and sniffed. Unless his nose was mistaken, and it rarely was where food was concerned, the kitchen was closed. A slow, satisfied grin spread across his face as he congratulated himself for pegging her reactions so correctly.

Rachel had always dealt with her problems by retreating until she'd either accepted the circumstances or thought of a way around them. Generally speaking, she hid behind a flurry of mind-numbing activity which could last for several hours or several days. The size of her project and the volume of the music she played while tackling her venture were directly proportional to the depth of her inner turmoil. He'd learned that her cleaning and tidying phases were for working small issues, like squabbles with her sisters or hurt feelings caused by insensitive friends, out of her system. For serious situations, she resorted to more ambitious construction projects. He still remembered the lemonade stand she'd tried to build from scrap lumber after her best friend had moved away.

Nick grinned as he pictured the structure she'd cobbled together. He'd volunteered to help but she'd refused his offer until she'd set a pitcher on the counter for the first time and it had collapsed like a house of cards.

In any event, tackling Hester's and Wilbur's house plainly indicated the gravity of her current internal conflict.

At the moment, from the pounding he heard through the open balcony door and the loud wail of the current song on the radio, Rachel definitely had created an atmosphere where few would feel welcome or want to linger.

He wasn't certain if he was being brave or foolish for trying to get a woman with a hammer in her hand to talk about her past, but he also knew that brooding indefinitely wouldn't help her at all. Whatever had soured her on her profession obviously included an ambulance, but regardless of what it was, he couldn't let her wallow in grief or guilt. Rachel was too special a person for him to leave her to her own devices and hope for the best. He simply had to get her to open up, which brought him full circle to his original dilemma.

Unfortunately, Rachel wouldn't be as easy to tease into unburdening herself as she used to be. His only option was to do the unexpected, which, under the circumstances, translated into pretending that this afternoon's incident had never happened. Unless, of course, he found the perfect lead into the conversation.

Balancing his load, Nick tried the knob and discovered she'd left the door unlocked. Without hesitation, he dumped the contents of his laundry bag into the washing machine in the mud room and started the wash cycle. Next, he stuffed the sweaty jug into her pathetically empty refrigerator, then followed the noise up the stairs.

He found Rachel in the far west bedroom, tearing off chunks of plasterboard with a vengeance. Everything about her, from her hair to her long-sleeved blue cotton shirt, denim shorts and her scuffed trainers, was covered in the same fine white dust that turned the air hazy.

He bent down to click off the radio and his ears thanked him. 'You're making good progress,' he commented.

She jumped in a startled reflex, simultaneously turning around to face him. Her eyes flashed with recognition as she pulled the mask off her nose and mouth, revealing a sheen of perspiration on her skin. Her shirt also showed damp patches, which didn't amaze him when he considered the temperature and distinct lack of air movement.

'I didn't hear you come in,' she said.

'I'm not surprised,' he said dryly, motioning to the walls. 'If you keep this up, we'll have the house ready for the market in record time.'

Rachel wiped her face on her long sleeve. 'Tearing down doesn't take as long as putting up.'

'You certainly don't have to be as careful,' he agreed,

glancing around the stud-exposed room. 'This corner of the house suffered the most water damage from the leaky roof, so I'm hoping we won't have to replace as much of the plasterboard in the other rooms.'

'I noticed the stains and crumbling walls,' she said, pointing at several areas. 'I assumed the roof had been the problem. What makes you think the rest of this floor isn't in the same condition?'

'I haven't seen any obvious signs of damage, but it still could exist. We won't know for certain until we steam off the wallpaper. I didn't bother with that step in here, because I could tell the walls had to be completely redone.'

He stepped close enough to pick off a suspicious white lump on the top of her head. 'Have you seen any termites?'

Her face blanched underneath the dirty rivulets of sweat and she jumped back. 'Termites?' she squeaked. 'There are *termites* in the house?'

Nick held out the clump of white plaster he'd removed from her hair. 'Not that I know of. I just wanted to know if you'd seen any. If you had, I'd call an exterminator first thing tomorrow.'

She stepped forward. 'You...you...weasel!' she ground out before she punched his shoulder.

'Hey, that hurt,' he said, surprised by the force.

'It should. You know how I hate bugs.'

'I thought maybe you'd grown out of your phobia.'

'Well, I hadn't.' She narrowed her eyes. '*Should* I be watching for termites?'

'We've already had the house inspected, so I think you're safe. The only pests you might run across are a mouse or two who've lost their way.'

'The only pest I've seen is the two-legged variety,' she said sweetly.

Nick laughed at her pointed reference. 'You always did know how to put me in my place.'

'Somebody had to.' Her gaze traveled over him. 'Are

you planning to work in your good clothes or are you only here for the view?'

He grinned wickedly. 'The view's great,' he said as he fixed his gaze on her long legs. 'I came by to throw a load of laundry in the washer and to see what your dinner menu was. I know we didn't set a time, but it is after six o'clock and I'm starved.'

'I didn't cook anything,' she said.

Hearing a combative note in her tone, he tried to sound as innocent as possible. 'Did I get the night wrong?'

'I lost track of time,' she said a trifle impatiently. 'Maybe tomorrow.'

Nick hid his smile. 'I thought you might forget,' he said, providing her with a plausible excuse, although he knew otherwise, 'so, I took the liberty of phoning in for pizza delivery. Our food should arrive in about ten minutes.'

'I'm really not hungry—' she began.

'If you're going to work like an entire construction crew, you need to eat,' Nick said sternly. 'When was the last time you stopped for a drink?'

'If you must know, it was about an hour ago. Give or take.'

'Make sure you don't get dehydrated,' he told her.

She planted her hands on her hips and glared at him. 'I can take care of myself.'

'I'm glad to hear it. I'd hate to admit you to the hospital because you collapsed from heat exhaustion.'

'You're not my doctor.'

'No, but your grandparents would support my decision if I felt a hospital stay was what you needed.'

'Look,' she said, 'I'm fine, and I know the hazards of working in the heat. Just go and enjoy your pizza. Better yet, feel free to share it with Andrea.'

A ray of hope pierced his chest. 'Do I detect the green-eyed monster?' he asked in a light tone to disguise his wishful thinking.

She rolled her eyes. 'Honestly. Where you get your ideas, I'll never know.'

'They pop in my head.'

'Sorry to disappoint you, Nick, but I never wanted to belong to anyone's fan club.'

'Ah. So you want a one-woman kind of guy.'

Her brown eyes seemed to turn darker. 'What's wrong with that?'

'Nothing. Does Charles fit your criteria?' He waited for her answer, hoping to hear a negative reply and afraid that he wouldn't.

'Yes, he does.'

'The question is, what will he do while you're here and he's there?'

'I trust him.'

'Trust is important in a relationship. Don't you agree?'

She rubbed the back of her neck. 'I really don't want to discuss this.'

'OK,' he said. 'We'll talk about something else while we're eating.'

Rachel's jaw seemed to tighten. 'I don't want to eat and I don't want to talk.'

'I seem to recall having this same argument yesterday. Are we having an instant replay?'

'Nick,' she said in a warning tone.

'OK, OK. We'll play by last night's rules. You don't have to eat if you don't want to. And if you don't want to talk, you can listen.'

'Listen to what?'

He shrugged. 'I'm never at a loss for words. I'll think of something.'

'You're not going to leave me alone, are you?'

'Not a chance,' he said cheerfully.

She chewed on her lower lip and he detected a slight slump to her previously stiff shoulders. She was wavering; Nick could feel the indecision rolling off her.

He tried to reassure her. 'I'm only asking you to grunt

once in a while so I know you're still awake. It's been a rough day and I need company.'

Her expression became sympathetic. 'What happened?'

'One of my patients went sour. He had kidney problems and went into renal failure this weekend.'

'Why didn't you transfer him to a dialysis unit?'

'He refused. He was ninety-two and had no family left. He wanted to go.'

'And you hung around and waited,' she said softly.

'It seemed the thing to do,' he said simply. The nurse on duty had called him early this morning to report Rufus Bell's deteriorating vital signs and he'd spent most of the day in the old gentleman's room so he wouldn't be alone when the end came.

Rachel motioned to the remaining section of wall. 'I'll stop, but I want to finish this first.'

He had been ready to haul her downstairs over one shoulder, but he was willing to compromise now that she had agreed. Another few minutes wouldn't matter.

'Okey-dokey,' he said, moving toward the pieces of wallboard lying on the floor. 'You tear down and I'll haul the trash outside.'

Once again, she eyed his navy blue trousers and white polo shirt. 'You'll get dirty.'

'That's what bathtubs and washing machines are for.' He clapped his hands. 'Hop to it, lady. I'm raring to go.'

By the time the delivery boy poked the doorbell, Rachel had pulled the rest of the plasterboard free and Nick had dropped the last pile of debris into the bin beneath the balcony.

'I'll shower while you start eating,' she told him.

Nick almost smiled at her stalling tactics. If he wasn't careful, she'd spend the evening in his comfortable apartment while he cooled his heels in her hot kitchen. 'I can wait another five minutes.'

'Five? It will take me that long to walk across the lawn.'

'All right, I'll give you fifteen, but if you take longer

than that, you won't get to try my raspberry lemonade. Construction work is thirsty work and I'm parched.'

Her face brightened. 'You made raspberry lemonade?'

'I *bought* it,' he corrected. 'I remembered how you loved lemonade and fresh raspberries, so I figured it was safe to assume you'd like the combination.'

'Absolutely.'

He gave her a gentle push to the door. 'Then go. Oh, and Rachel?'

Her steps slowed. 'Yes?'

'Just so you know… If you're not back soon, I'll come after you.'

'Bossy as ever, aren't you?'

His answering grin as he tapped the face of his watch sent her scurrying through the door.

As soon as she'd disappeared, Nick mentally patted himself on the back. Even if he didn't accomplish anything else tonight, he could take pride in one thing. He'd brought a smile to her face and put a spring in her step.

CHAPTER FIVE

RACHEL relaxed on the chaise longue and sipped her third glass of raspberry lemonade as she focused on the view from the front porch. She hadn't wanted company and still didn't, but having Nick sprawled nearby on a chair identical to hers hadn't turned out quite as bad as she'd anticipated. In fact, his presence was almost comforting. For a while, she could pretend that she was carefree and had nothing more worrisome on her mind than how to spend this beautiful, if hot summer evening.

Nick had stuck to his word and did most of the talking while he ate. She listened, at least during those few minutes when her own thoughts didn't wander in other directions.

On the surface, their time together seemed innocent. A handsome man had shown up on her doorstep, convinced her to take a break and now they were sitting on the porch in each other's company, enjoying a nice night.

She knew better than to think Nick's arrival and pizza invitation were as innocent as they appeared. His uncanny ability to sense when she was preoccupied clearly hadn't diminished over the years they'd drifted apart. Soon he would steer the conversation around to the ER episode.

If she had any sense, she'd go ahead and tell him what had happened. Nick wasn't the type to leave the proverbial sleeping dogs to lie, and so he'd eventually discover her secrets. She hated to have her failures paraded in front of him and then suffer through his inevitable critique. On the other hand, perhaps he'd be so repulsed by what she'd done that he'd leave her to her solitude.

'Don't you agree?' he asked.

His question reeled her back from the path she had traveled. 'Sorry. What did you say?'

He grinned. 'Wool-gathering?'

'Just wondering what walls I'll attack next,' she prevaricated.

'We'll have to remove the wallpaper first,' he reminded her. 'No sense in knocking off plaster if we don't need to.'

'Is that a hint as to what you want me to do tomorrow?'

'Unless you can replace sheet-rock by yourself.'

'It's a two-man job and you know it.'

He grinned. 'Then we'll save it for a day when I'll be here to help.'

'Steaming wallpaper. Sounds like a fun thing to do in the heat,' she said dryly. 'Are you going to tell me what room to start with, or can I choose for myself?'

His smile grew wider as if he found the petulance in her voice amusing. 'I'll let you make the decision.'

'Gee, thanks.' She rubbed both sides of her neck to alleviate the stiffness, feeling each and every muscle she hadn't used before. Grimacing at the pain in her shoulders, across her back and down her arms, she shifted position and vowed to take things easier for the next few days.

'Sore?' he asked.

'A little. I guess I'm not as prepared for strenuous physical activity as I thought I was.'

'Good thing I stopped you when I did,' he said, finishing the last slice of ham and pineapple pizza. 'You'd have knocked out plaster until you needed physical therapy.'

'Maybe,' she said, although she knew he was right. She'd been so mired in the past that she hadn't paid attention to her body's signs of protest.

'There's no maybe about it,' he said. 'I've worked with a lot of guys and, from what I saw, you would have run rings around any of them.'

'Don't be silly.'

'I'm serious,' he insisted. 'You were a one-woman

wrecking crew. Are you always going to work this hard, or was today an exception?'

Rachel sipped more of her drink, wondering if he'd use this as his opening for the episode in the ER. 'I wanted to accomplish a lot this weekend, so I thought I'd better get busy.'

'You certainly did.' He grinned. 'Think you can hammer a nail as good as you can punch a hole?'

'Just watch me,' she said.

'I'll look forward to it. After seeing you struggle with the lemonade stand when we were twelve—'

'I was just learning, so you can't hold my incompetence against me.' She remembered that week well. As traumatic events went, it had ranked with some of her worst and she had felt utterly lost. 'Unlike you, there are some of us who can't do everything perfectly the first time.'

He straightened. 'Where did you get an idea like that?'

Rachel couldn't believe the surprise in his voice. 'Come, now,' she said. 'You forget how many summers we spent together. You sailed through everything you did.'

He appeared incredulous. 'Do you honestly believe that nonsense?'

'Absolutely. For example, what about baseball? You were the best player on the field and my grandfather has the newspaper articles to prove it. Then there was soccer. Tennis, too, if I recall.'

Nick shrugged. 'Athletics came easily for me.'

'What about your other activities? Grams told me how you ran for student council in school and won by a landslide. And that summer job at the pool? Everyone wanted it, including me, but who got hired? You did. And you couldn't even swim at the time!'

He laughed. 'If you'll recall, I wasn't a lifeguard. I ran the concession stand and wasn't allowed to get in the water.'

'Then why did you want the position?'

'Get real, Rach. What thirteen-year-old boy wouldn't

want to be where he could check out the high-school babes in their swimsuits?'

'Really? With all the girls flocking around you and asking me how to attract your attention, you shouldn't have needed to look further afield.'

He chuckled. 'Looking is half the fun. As for the student council, I campaigned hard for my position.'

'So you passed out a lot of "Vote for Nick" flyers,' she said, dismissing his argument. 'So did your friends. The point is, Nick, you've never failed at anything in your life.'

His smile died. 'That's not true,' he said quietly.

'Tell me one thing that you wanted desperately but didn't get.'

'I could name several.'

'One. I only want one,' she insisted.

'There was this girl,' he began.

Rachel was incredulous. 'You're telling me that one of your failures involved a *girl*?'

He straightened, appearing affronted. 'What's so strange about that?'

'Nothing, other than you always attracted females like sugar draws ants.'

'I didn't want a colony,' he said. 'I only wanted to take one particular young lady on a date. Alone.'

'You couldn't get her alone?' Rachel cringed at the shriek in her voice. 'Mr I-know-all-the-shortcuts-to-lovers'-lane?'

'My reputation was greatly exaggerated.'

She scoffed. 'What was her name? I'd like to know who was able to resist your charms.'

He shot her an exasperated glare. 'It's confidential.'

At Rachel's hoot of laughter, he added, 'Do you want to hear this or not?'

'Sorry.'

'We were friends, but she never acted as if she'd wanted our relationship to be anything more, shall we say, romantic.'

Her curiosity piqued, Rachel found herself affronted on Nick's behalf. 'You had lots of female friends. Which one was she?' she demanded. 'Some blonde bimbo without two brain cells to rub together. Susie Patterson, right?'

'It wasn't Susie. Don't bother to ask me her name again because I won't tell you.'

Something in his voice told her that she'd touched a sore spot. Rachel swung her legs over the edge of the chaise longue and sat with her elbows propped on her knees. Having suffered her own secret crush, she could empathize. 'Didn't you ever let her know how you felt? Or ask her out?'

'I tried, but...' He shook his head. 'I was afraid she'd laugh at me. I didn't want to lose what we had, so I kept things platonic. I came close a few times—tried to kiss her twice—but I made a mess out of every chance I had.'

'I find that hard to believe.'

'It's true. Is she still local?' Rachel asked.

'Yeah.'

'How do you feel about her now?'

He didn't answer at first, but when he did he gave her a boyish grin. 'I'd like to see if we could start a blaze. The problem is, I'm not sure she's available.'

Rachel rolled her eyes. 'She either is or she isn't. There's no such thing as being half-available. Is she engaged?'

'No. At least I don't think so.'

'You've always been a man of action,' Rachel told him. 'If she's not made any commitments to this other fellow, take my advice and go for it.'

'What if she's not interested?'

Rachel stretched a new kink out of her shoulder. 'I can't believe you're asking me this question. What woman wouldn't be interested in Nick Sheridan, MD? You've got everything going for you. A promising future, a good practice, a wonderful personality—'

'An old car, enough debts to rival the gross national

product and an apartment that's hardly the height of luxury.'

She waved his objections aside. 'Those are just *things* and they're temporary. Everybody has old cars and loans when they're starting out. They have nothing to do with the real *you*. The guy who rescued baby birds, who helped rebuild my lemonade stand and who, when he was fourteen, spearheaded the aluminum can fund drive for that little boy with cancer is the man any woman would be thrilled to come home to every night. And if your mystery lady doesn't realize what a jewel you are, then you're better off without her!'

A slow grin crossed his face. 'You know something? You do wonders for my ego.'

'I'm only telling the truth,' she insisted.

He leaned back. 'What about you? Any unrequited love interest in your past?'

Rachel laughed. 'As a matter of fact, yes.' She spoke nonchalantly to keep him from guessing. 'He was kind and thoughtful and very protective. And he treated me like his sister.'

'He was an idiot.'

She smiled, wondering if he'd say the same thing if he knew that *he* was the one she was talking about. 'Yeah.'

'Sounds like we both struck out in the relationship department. I'll bet we've had similar professional failures, too. Want to hear one of mine?'

'Not really.'

He clearly didn't listen because he started his story. 'I had a little guy during my pediatrics rotation. Cuter than the dickens. The only problem was, we had a horrible time trying to control his seizures. We used every anti-epileptic drug available, but nothing worked. I watched him go from this happy, smiling child to one who didn't respond to stimuli of any kind. He eventually—'

Rachel stood, too nervous to sit. 'I don't want to hear this.'

'I always thought we should have been able to do more, but we couldn't. Medicine doesn't have all the answers.'

A familiar knot formed in her chest, the same knot that made it difficult to breathe. 'You've been waiting to share your words of wisdom and your platitudes all night, haven't you?'

'I only took advantage of the opportunity,' he said. 'I'm sure you saw your own share of tragedy. You can't work in this profession and be insulated from it.'

'Which is why I'm not a nurse any more.'

'How can you say that?' he asked. 'If you've been trained, it doesn't matter whether you're using your knowledge or not. You are a nurse and have the same abilities you had before.'

'You don't know the situation.'

'No, I don't,' he said. 'But I'd like to.'

She moved to stand near the railing and clutched her glass like a talisman. 'We were discussing you, not me.'

'Turn about's fair play. Besides, you know I won't tell a soul. Did I ever breathe a word to your grandparents about why your sink started leaking quite mysteriously?'

Rachel remembered that day well. She'd found Amy's diary and had locked herself in the bathroom to read it. Unfortunately, Rachel had accidentally dropped the key down the drain and she'd commandeered Nick to help her retrieve it. By the time they'd finished and the key had been safely back in Amy's hiding place, the sink had looked the same as before. However, appearances had been deceptive and shortly afterwards her grandfather had to call a plumber.

'No, you didn't,' she admitted.

'And did I ever tell Marta how you'd sneak out the window and climb down the tree to go to the movies with me when she was babysitting and you were supposed to be in bed?'

'No, but only because you would have gotten into trouble, too.'

'That's beside the point. And did I ever tell a soul about the incident involving—?'

Rachel waved her free hand. 'I get the picture. It's not that I'm afraid you'll tell anyone…'

An air of expectancy hung between them as she avoided Nick's gaze. Tracing a bead of moisture down the side of her glass, she said softly. 'People expect us to do the impossible. *We* expect it of ourselves, too, and it's a bitter pill when we slip off our pedestals.'

'Ambulances don't always bring in people who can be saved,' he said quietly.

'No, they don't.'

'Whether their conditions are by accident or by choice, we can only do our best and accept that there are times when our best simply isn't good enough.'

Rachel glanced at him. 'But what if we didn't do our best?'

He frowned. 'I don't understand.'

'What if someone died because you didn't do your best,' she said. 'How do you accept that?'

'You can't second-guess yourself, Rachel. I'm sure you did what you could at the time.'

She turned her head to stare into the distance. 'I froze, Nick. That's not doing what I could have, or should have.'

He sounded cautious. 'Everyone reacts differently to situations.'

'I've handled more car-accident victims than I can even begin to count. I've seen a lot of gruesome ones—detached limbs, crushed chests, head injuries so bad that we couldn't believe how they'd stayed alive long enough to be transported—and I always, *always* held myself together and did my job without batting an eyelash.'

'What was different about this case?'

Rachel drew a deep breath before she courageously fixed her attention on him to watch his reaction. 'She was my friend and I didn't help her. Or her daughter.'

She expected to see a flash of censure, even distaste in

Nick's eyes, but instead of condemnation she saw sympathy. For a moment she didn't know which response was worse.

Finally, he shook his head, his gaze never leaving hers. 'I know you and I can't believe the picture is as bad as you're painting it to be.'

'Take my word for it,' she said dryly.

'Why don't you let me be the judge?'

Rachel drew a deep breath and related what had happened that horrible night from memory. 'The ambulance brought in a woman with massive chest injuries and a child with head trauma. I met both stretchers at the door, saw the blood pooling underneath the little girl's head and watched her go into a seizure that wouldn't stop. I could tell from the doctor's expression that she didn't have a chance. So he sent me to help the other victim.

'I remember thinking that the shirt she wore—or what was left of it—was identical to the one I'd bought my friend for her birthday. It wasn't until the doctor intubated her that I realized it was Grace. Then I knew it was her daughter Molly in the next bed. By then she'd slipped into a coma and died within the next few minutes.

'All I could think of was that this wasn't supposed to happen. Grace and Holling were getting married the next week and she and Molly were driving back from seeing her parents. I found out later that some kids were joyriding in a pickup and when they ran a stop sign on a country road because they'd been drinking, they plowed into Grace's little Geo. According to the EMTs who brought them in, they had to use the jaws of life to extract them from what was left of the car.'

'So once you recognized Grace, you—'

'I froze,' she said flatly. 'I literally couldn't function. The doctor had to push me aside so another nurse could take my place. She was new, not as experienced, and nervous. They wasted precious minutes trying to stabilize Grace. If

I'd had my wits about me, they would have gotten her up-stairs to surgery sooner. They would have saved her.'

'You don't know that,' he said calmly. 'It sounds as if her injuries were too severe.'

'The doctor said that if they got her to surgery in time, she had a chance. *A chance* that I blew because I let my emotions interfere with my responsibilities.'

'It wouldn't have made a difference, Rachel.'

His quiet words didn't make her feel any better. 'What sort of team leader am I if I can't function in an emergency? In *any* emergency?'

'Grace was your friend. You lost your objectivity for a minute or two. No one faults you for that.'

'I do. We're trained to be objective. To not let our personal feelings intrude.' She rubbed the back of her neck, accepting the pain caused by strained muscles as her penance.

'The scenario you described is every ER person's nightmare. Don't you think everyone worries about seeing a loved one arrive in an ambulance?'

'That may be, but how many of them would freeze like I did? After that, I was afraid every time the bay doors opened for fear it would be someone else I knew.'

'Were there any accusations made? Charges leveled?'

'N-no.'

'What did the autopsy show?'

She'd made a point of finding out. 'A lacerated aorta, punctured lung, internal injuries.'

'And you believe that in those ten seconds it took for another nurse to take over, you made the difference between your friend living and dying? Sorry, but I don't buy that. I'm not just saying that to make you feel better either.'

Nick wasn't telling her anything that she hadn't heard from various other people, including the head of ER and her director of nursing. Unfortunately, her heart told her differently.

'Your friend could have died from any *one* of those

causes,' Nick continued. 'Add them together and she basically needed a miracle.'

'Yes, but—'

'Unless you're in the miracle business, and I think you're just as human as the rest of us, those few seconds didn't affect the final outcome.'

'Maybe not,' she reluctantly admitted, 'but after that we had a string of horrible cases—a six-year-old shot in a drive-by shooting, a stabbing victim, a baby showing signs of definite abuse. None of them survived and I couldn't deal with the stress any more.'

'So you came to Hooper to hide.'

'To sort myself out,' she corrected. 'To re-establish my goals.'

'We can't fix every medical condition,' he said. 'It's unfortunate, but you have to accept that fact.'

Rachel fell silent as his words hammered home the same truth everyone else had tried to give her. She offered a tremulous smile. 'My head has a tendency to agree, but my heart doesn't. And I don't know what to do about it.'

'The cure for falling off a horse is to get back on.'

Nick made it sound so easy, but it wasn't. 'What if I fall off again? What if someone else I know comes in and I freeze again?'

'And what if you don't?' he countered.

She crossed her arms, feeling cold in spite of the temperature. 'I can't risk it. I won't.'

'You can't run for ever. Those incidents with the Pearson boy and Jack Rexton should have shown you that. You handled their problems like the pro you are. Dylan would give his eye-teeth for you to work in his department.'

'I wasn't in the ER and an ambulance wasn't involved,' she pointed out.

'Our emergency department doesn't see the case mix that you did. We don't have the same level of excitement or stress.'

'That may be true, but look at how I reacted when an

ambulance *did* roll in. Until I know that I can function under any circumstances, I wouldn't do anyone any good.'

'Don't sell yourself short, Rachel. If you don't want to cover ER, there are other areas in the hospital that could use your skills.'

She drew a tremulous breath. 'Working on this house is the only job I'm interested in at the moment. Please, accept my decision as final.'

He opened his mouth as if he intended to argue, then closed it. 'If you need breathing space, you've got it.'

'Thanks.' She hadn't realized how rigidly she'd held herself until the muscles in her shoulders cramped. Trying to relieve the pain, she massaged the area as far as she could reach.

'Come on,' he said as he approached her. 'Let's go inside.'

'What for? It's cooler out here.'

'That may be, but the bugs are starting to make their presence known. And for what I intend to do, I suspect you'd prefer privacy.'

'Privacy? What do you have in mind?'

He nodded. 'There are small children in the neighborhood and I don't think you'll want them to see you without your shirt on.'

'Take off my shirt?' she faltered.

'Sure. You can't have a decent back rub with it on. Do you have any witch hazel?'

A *back rub*? The thought of Nick's hands running across her skin, kneading her muscles, teasing her nerve endings, was enough to make her heart fibrillate and her lungs deflate. 'Sorry. It's really not necessary.'

'If I don't take out the kinks, you're going to be stiffer than a board tomorrow.'

'Yes, well, it wouldn't be the first time.'

'You always were stubborn.' As she opened her mouth to complain, he added, 'Don't fuss. You know you can't win. I outrank you.'

'Outrank me?' she said. 'How?'

'I'm the foreman of this project, in case you've forgotten.'

'We agreed to work together. Partners,' she reminded him. 'No decisions would be made until we discussed them first.'

'True, but do you have actual construction experience?' At her negative headshake, he added, 'Plus, I'm the on-site medical authority.'

'Says who?'

His eyes shone with merriment. 'If this was poker, you'd have to agree that my MD beats your RN any day.' He pulled her to the door. 'Go on in and turn on the fan while I dash home for my liniment. And would you mind tossing my clothes in the dryer?'

'Anything else?' she asked sarcastically. 'Sew on a few buttons, clean your house or—' The phrase 'bear your children' dropped into her head but she managed to keep from blurting it out. She thought quickly for a substitution. 'Iron your shirts?'

His grin was the same endearing, lopsided one that had sent her teenage heart into handsprings. Her adult heart suffered the same symptoms.

'Cookies would be nice,' he said. 'My sweet tooth's been bothering me.'

'The kitchen is closed until further notice.'

Nick snapped his fingers. 'Darn. Do you think it will reopen soon?'

'Maybe your flavor of the month will take pity on you.' At his frown, she added, 'Remember Andrea?'

He waved his hand. 'She doesn't know the difference between a mixer and a potato masher.'

'What a shame. Better luck with your next girlfriend.'

'I can hope. I'm curious, though. What did you mean by your flavor-of-the-month comment?'

'According to my grandad, you know most, if not all of the single ladies in town.'

He laughed. 'I don't think they'd appreciate your description. Don't worry, once I've found the right one, I'll be just as staid as your Charles.'

Before she could correct him, he vaulted over the railing onto the ground below like an experienced gymnast.

Shaking her head at his daring for not taking the steps, Rachel watched him disappear around the side of the house. Charles certainly would never have done anything so foolhardy but, then, he wasn't as athletic as Nick. As for being staid, Charles *was* more introverted, but that only meant he was different. At least she didn't have to worry about him dumping her because another woman had caught his eye.

Realizing that Nick would return and find her standing on the porch if she didn't stop daydreaming, she went inside. The living room sofa seemed the most comfortable place other than her own bed, but she wasn't about to let his fingers walk up and down her spine *there*. It was hard enough to keep her attraction toned down to a scale he wouldn't notice. Sharing a mattress with him, even under innocent circumstances, would make it impossible.

She plugged in the small fan and pointed it in the sofa's direction. Then, because she was thirsty, she refilled their cups with fresh ice and the last of the lemonade he'd provided. He still hadn't returned, so she went into the mud room and began loading his wet clothes in the dryer.

As she shook out the wrinkles on a blue knit shirt, the scent clinging to the cloth made it seem as if Nick were standing next to her. She breathed deeply, wishing for his arms to be around her instead of soggy fabric.

'I found it,' Nick said triumphantly as he entered and caught her by surprise.

'Good. Good,' she finished lamely, emptying the washer in record time before she slammed the dryer door closed and twisted the knob with a flourish.

'Thanks for doing that,' he said. 'I'll do the same for you some time.'

'Sure,' she said, eager to agree to anything if it meant

they would leave the mud room before he realized she'd been practically drooling over his clothes.

'Are you ready?'

'Yeah, well, I've been thinking,' she said, unable to stop him from shooing her into the living room. 'My muscles are feeling better. They're not as tight as they were earlier.'

Nick raised one expressive dark eyebrow. 'I know you don't like pain, Rach, but this isn't a nasty medical procedure. It's a massage and it's going to feel good. Trust me.' He wiggled his fingers.

'Feeling good is the problem,' she muttered.

'Did you say something?' he asked.

'No. Let's get on with this.' She plunked herself face down on the sofa, burying her face in the throw pillow and steeling herself for his touch.

'Uh, Rach?' he asked, settling on the edge with his hip against hers, effectively pinning her against the back of the sofa.

'What?' she said, her voice muffled.

'The liniment will work better if it doesn't have to soak through your shirt before it hits the skin.'

'Oh.' Her face warmed at least ten degrees above boiling as she sat up, yanked the T-shirt over her head and fought the urge to hide the lacy strips of fabric she called a bra from his view. Because of the unisex uniforms she'd worn for years, she'd indulged herself with the sexiest silk and lace undergarments in the wildest colors she could find in lingerie shops. Wearing decadent lingerie underneath her shapeless scrub suits did wonders for a girl's mental health.

Unfortunately, *knowing* she had a sinfully wicked black wisp of lace against her skin was different than *modeling* it to a member of the opposite sex. As nonchalantly as possible, she turned her back, spread her shirt on the rough tweed sofa cushion and lay face down once again, grateful that Nick wouldn't see how her face had taken on the hues of sunburn.

'Much better.' His note of satisfaction sounded as clear as church bells on a summer Sunday morning.

Rachel didn't move a muscle. 'Are you going to get started or not?'

'Of course. Now, just relax.'

The cool lotion slathered on his hand nearly sent her into orbit. 'Hey,' he said, his voice filled with humor, 'you're wound tighter than a spring.'

She settled back down. 'Sorry. I'm just not used…to this.'

'To what? Having someone rub your back?'

Having *a man* rub her back. 'Yeah,' she answered.

'You mean Chandler hasn't taken time to tickle your spine?'

'Charles,' she corrected. 'And, no, he hasn't.' Her admission came reluctantly and with some regret. There had been occasions when a back rub would have helped her unwind from a stressful day, but he'd never volunteered and she'd never asked.

Nick bent down far enough for his breath to caress her ear. 'I'm glad I'm the first.'

Before she could reply, his fingers dug into a sore spot and she yelped. 'Easy,' he said as he kneaded the area until the pain became pleasure and she grunted in response.

For the next several minutes, he addressed every inch of her back from her neck down to her waist. As he worked on her arms, his knuckles brushed against the sides of her breasts but she was too relaxed to do anything but revel in the sensations he'd created.

Moans slipped out of her mouth as he addressed the aches she'd earned, but she couldn't say at what point the sounds began to signal pure and utter enjoyment. Her skin tingled as if electrified and each stroke of his fingers, each feather-light caress seemed to stir something primal inside her.

Her entire body quivered as if waiting…waiting for his fingers to progress to other, more sensitive areas. She had no idea how long he worked his magic. He was surely tired, but she couldn't summon the strength to ask him to stop.

The dryer buzzed and the harsh noise was so out of place that she instantly came out of her haze and flopped onto her back. His hands had been massaging her shoulder blades, but they now rested firmly on her breasts.

For a long moment she didn't move, noticing that he didn't either. His eyes gleamed with delight before he moved his hands in seeming slow motion to rest on her waist.

'The clothes are done,' she said inanely, feeling a trail of heat down the path his fingers had taken.

'So I hear,' he said, making no move to rise.

'You have wonderful hands,' she said. 'If you ever give up your doctor's diploma, you can make a fortune in physical therapy.'

His gaze was intent, although his voice retained a teasing quality. 'I could always start moonlighting. What would you pay for a session?'

'As good as I feel, you could name your price.'

'Anything?'

His expression became speculative and she became afraid of what he'd ask and even more so of what he *wouldn't*. If nothing else, she was one hundred per cent certain that after this evening he'd finally stop looking at her as if she were one of his sisters.

'Anything within reason.' Her words came out in a husky whisper.

'Then,' he drawled, 'I want a kiss.'

CHAPTER SIX

NICK fixed his gaze upon Rachel. If he looked anywhere other than her face, especially at the little scrap of fabric that revealed more than it covered, he wouldn't have taken time to ask her anything. As it was, his body was already miles ahead of where it should be at this stage in the game and it wouldn't require much provocation for him to explode.

'A kiss?' she asked, sounding surprised.

He nodded, dimly realizing that the obnoxious background buzz had stopped. 'A toe-curling, hair-raising, let's-forget-about-the-world kiss.'

Her smile inched its way across her face and her eyes shone with pleasure. 'I'd like that.'

Her shyness reminded him to take things slowly, but as soon as he leaned over and his lips touched hers, his plans flew out the window.

She tasted like warm honey and felt soft and snuggly in his arms. He couldn't refrain from stroking her smooth skin, entranced by the physical differences between them.

He rapidly shifted position so they were both lying on the sofa, their arms and legs entwined. Hearing her reaction to his touch with those little sounds in her throat made his chest swell until he thought his buttons would burst. Rachel had responded to *him*. Whatever her relationship with Charles, the sparks between her and himself should tell her something.

Perhaps he should feel guilty for his actions when he knew she had another man in her life, but Rachel herself had encouraged him to press his suit. And he intended to do exactly as she'd ordered.

He touched her from the top of her head, tracing a line down to her waist. He tasted her lips, nibbled on her ear lobe and kissed a path to between her breasts. Her airy floral fragrance seemed to fill his every pore and her breathy sounds of delight were music to his ears. Rachel had somehow enhanced every sense he possessed, and the knowledge reinforced what he was now beginning to suspect. Rachel could easily be more than a friend.

He felt every move she made, noticing how her own touch was like a butterfly caress as she ran her hands over his face, down his neck and arms. His body ached for more as she tugged his shirt from his waistband and wormed her fingers underneath the fabric until finally she placed her palm against his bare chest.

The dryer buzzed again and this time Rachel slowly broke away from his searching mouth. 'Your clothes will wrinkle if we don't hang them up.'

'Who cares?' he said, nuzzling her neck. He didn't want these few moments to end.

She chuckled. 'You will when your patients wonder why you look rumpled.'

'It wouldn't be the first time,' he said. Although the spell had been broken, enough magic lingered in the air to re-kindle the flames. 'That was quite a kiss, by the way.'

Rachel pulled her hand out of his shirt. 'Then I assume my debt is paid?'

'For now.'

'For now?' The husky quality of her voice did strange things to the blood flowing to a certain portion of his anatomy.

'If you're paying with kisses, I'm hoping you'll need another back rub soon.'

She smiled but didn't answer.

He tested the waters. 'If you kiss Charlton like that, I'm surprised he lets you out of his sight.'

Rachel's grin slowly faded. Her movements as she sat up were jerky, and if he hadn't moved with her he would have landed on his backside. Her face stony, she slipped her shirt over her head and finger-combed her hair.

'His name is *Charles*. And if you were trying to prove something—'

'I wasn't. I wanted to kiss you. I didn't think about Chauncey until…later.' Nick wasn't about to say that her response had given him hope. Surely she would realize that if Charles couldn't knock her proverbial socks off like he himself just had, then Charles wasn't the man for her.

The fire in Rachel's eyes faded. 'He and I…' She hesitated. 'We are…' Once again, she didn't finish. Nick suspected that she couldn't.

'Comfortable?' he suggested.

'Yes. We get along very well. We have the same tastes and interests and we never argue.'

'About anything?'

'About anything,' she reiterated. 'We have a pleasant relationship.'

It sounded boring to Nick, but he kept his comment to himself. He couldn't see a Rachel who'd shimmied down a tree in order to sneak out of the house willing to settle for such a placid existence. If he couldn't talk to her about her nursing career, maybe he could get her to reconsider how she wanted to spend the next fifty years or so of her life.

After all, Nick had the advantage. He was here and dear old Charlie wasn't.

'I'm sorry I can't make it to Hooper like I'd planned,' Charles told Rachel two Fridays later. 'We're installing the interface for a new piece of lab equipment and we've already run into problems. I'm going to spend the weekend working.'

Because Nick was standing within listening distance of the upstairs hallway phone, Rachel clutched the receiver in her hand and tried to disguise her disappointment. 'I understand, but I'd really hoped to show you around. We've accomplished a lot these past couple of weeks.'

'This interface is important. I can't just take off for a road trip.'

She turned her back to Nick and spoke softly. 'You're not a one-man department. There are other people who can deal with this.'

'Rachel, you know I don't ask my staff to do what I wouldn't do myself.'

She sighed. 'I know.'

'There will be other weekends,' he said pragmatically.

Forcing a lighter note, she said, 'You're right. There will be.' She knew how Charles thrived on solving computer problems, but would he ever rank her higher than a computer chip?

'How's it going with the guy who's helping you? Nate, I believe.'

Rachel wondered why both Nick and Charles had trouble referring to each other. Charles had an excuse. He barely remembered his own employees', much less someone he hadn't met. Nick, however, had always been a whiz with people's names. Suffering from such blatant memory lapses now simply indicated that he'd developed his aggravating new habit to tease her.

'Nick,' she corrected.

'Whatever.' He sounded impatient and Rachel imagined a matching expression on his face. 'Is he a help or a hindrance?'

Rachel hesitated. How could she describe what it was like to have Nick around? She couldn't deny that he'd been invaluable in terms of expertise and knowledge. His presence, however, was bittersweet. It was nice having another person to talk to while she worked, but at the same time she couldn't get his kiss out of her mind. Every time he smiled at her or touched her in any way, she felt as if her temperature had risen another degree.

Unfortunately, her reactions troubled her to no end and

she wanted to slug Nick for placing her in the untenable position of having Charles and wanting Nick instead. Her sorry state brought her to the real reason why she'd practically begged Charles to visit. If he were here, he could act as a buffer and lay her strange feelings to rest.

Then again, perhaps Nick would make Charles jealous and he'd become a little more attentive.

'Both,' she said.

'What do you mean by that? He's either pulling his weight or he's not.'

'He's definitely pulling his weight,' she answered.

'Then what's the problem?'

How like Charles to look at everything as black or white, without any shades of gray. 'None, really,' she said, wishing she hadn't said a word. She couldn't very well explain how the problem wasn't with Nick *per se*, but with her.

'We're having minor differences of opinion,' she added.

'Is that all?' He sounded both relieved and disgusted, as if he clearly considered their opposing ideas inconsequential.

'Afraid so,' she said. 'Nothing to worry about.'

'I won't. I'll call you when I get the situation here under control.'

Rachel knew that could occur tomorrow or in two weeks. One point in Charles's favor was that he never made promises he couldn't keep. Now that she thought about it, he rarely promised anything in the first place.

'I'll be here.' She disconnected the call and hesitated a moment before she re-entered the room where Nick was sitting on the floor to clean his nail gun.

'We need to fix that squeaky floorboard,' she said.

'In due time,' Nick promised as he lumbered to his feet. 'How're things with Chester?'

'*Charles*,' she corrected automatically. 'He's fine.'

'Is he coming this weekend?'

Rachel stuffed a handful of masonry nails into the carpenter's pouch at her waist. 'He's installing an interface and can't leave because it's not doing what it's supposed to.'

Nick frowned. 'He's a manager, isn't he?'

'Yes.'

'Then doesn't his staff deal with those problems?'

'He likes to work alongside his people,' Rachel said, quoting Charles's favorite line. 'He doesn't ask his employees to do something that he's not willing to do himself. In this case, it means giving up his weekend.'

'Carter sounds like quite a guy.'

This time, she didn't bother to correct him. 'He is.'

'What do you say we make our own plans?'

She glanced at him. 'I doubt if Andrea wants a threesome.'

'She's seeing someone else.'

'You broke up?'

'There wasn't anything between us to break.'

'But I thought—'

'We were an item?' At her nod, he continued, 'Sorry to disappoint you, but we weren't. She had her eyes set on a certain occupational therapist.'

'You're kidding.'

'No, I'm not. So what do you say to playing hooky tomorrow evening for a drive to Joplin?'

She was tempted. 'But there's so much to do yet.'

'Look at how much you've already accomplished,' he said, motioning with his arms. 'Come on, Rach. One night won't make that much difference. You'll burn out if you don't pace yourself. Besides, after we finish taping the seams, we'll be ready for the next phase.'

The idea of taking a night off appealed to her. After spending the past ten days steaming and scraping wallpaper, patching walls and sanding the dried putty to create a smooth surface, she deserved a reward. They also had to decide on whether to paint, wallpaper or do both, so now was a good time for a breather.

'What would we do?' she asked, immediately thinking

of all of the hotels in the area because of the highly traveled interstate. *Get a grip*, she scolded herself.

'There's a great Greek restaurant you'd like. It's called Arde's Villa.'

Rachel thought for a moment. 'I don't remember it. Must be new.'

'It's a few years old,' he said. 'Arde renovated the Reding's Mill swimming pool. The bath house is the restaurant and the pool is now a garden.'

'I remember the pool,' she said excitedly. 'It had the neatest water slides. Everyone loved to swim there because it was so different from Hooper's. I hated to hear it had closed.'

'Now it's a hot-spot for fine dining.' He eyed her brown shorts and beige-colored vest. 'You'll need to dress up.'

She'd only packed casual clothes but had thrown a denim skirt in her suitcase at the last minute. However, she wanted an outfit more dazzling than denim for her fairy-tale evening—something silky, maybe even clingy. Hooper had a small but well-stocked clothing store downtown that surely would carry the dress she had in mind.

'It's a date.' Once she'd spoken, she realized Nick could assume she was pushing romantic overtones on his offer so she backpedaled. To describe their evening in such a way seemed disloyal to Charles. 'I mean, it's not a date in the true sense of the word. It's a—'

'Date,' he said firmly. 'We're going out to have a good time, so don't get caught up in semantics.'

She smiled. 'All right.' Straightening her shoulders, she reached for the putty knife. 'If we're taking tomorrow off, we'd better get busy and finish. I want to go to Bates' for the wall-covering books before they close.'

He groaned. 'Tonight?'

'Tonight,' she repeated. 'Unless you're willing to give me carte blanche on decorating.'

'Not a chance,' he said, his eyes gleaming. 'I don't want

the guy who buys this house for his family to face pink flowers everywhere he goes.'

'I won't put pink flowers in every room,' she retorted. 'Only in the bedroom.'

Nick groaned and melodramatically covered his eyes with his arm. 'Have pity on the guy.'

'What about his significant other and her preferences?'

'Maybe she likes less girlie stuff, too. I dated a woman once who absolutely hated pastel colors and floral prints.'

'She's an exception.'

'Maybe not.'

'The point is, we have to decorate for a broad appeal.'

'Exactly.' His grin was triumphant.

'Now we simply have to define what appeals to the most people.'

His gaze narrowed. 'How do you intend to do that? We don't have time to conduct a poll.'

'We don't,' she agreed. 'But the salespeople at Bates' certainly know which patterns sell the best. Do you agree to accept what they recommend?'

'*If*, and that's a big if, it isn't a high-school student, I'll agree to *consider* their opinion.'

'What's wrong with a high-school student?'

'Nothing. Other than I don't think a kid who has purple hair and rings in his nose can give me sound advice on home decor.'

'Your prejudice is showing.'

'Yeah, well, when he recommends neon yellow walls and black lights for special effects, we'll see who's right.'

Rachel doubted whether the situation at Bates' would come close to the one Nick had described. The moment she saw the teenage girl behind the counter, her hair a strange sort of orange with purple highlights, she knew she'd lost any ground she might have gained.

Nick leaned over to whisper in Rachel's ear, 'Do you really think she knows what appeals to conservative folks?'

'I'm keeping an open mind.'

The girl glanced up from the stack of invoices in front of her and gave them a bright smile. 'May I help you?'

'Not likely,' Nick muttered under his breath.

Rachel elbowed him in his side and smiled at the girl—'Caroline,' her badge stated. 'We'd like to look at your wall-covering books.'

Caroline motioned to the long counter where the portfolios were stacked in haphazard array. Several bar stools stood nearby so that customers could rest the books on the counter-top and sit while scanning the contents. 'Help yourself. If you want to take any home, just fill out the card on the inside pocket. We have a limit of four books per customer and they're due back within forty-eight hours.'

'Thanks,' Rachel answered.

'Are you interested in anything in particular?'

Nick interrupted. 'Not really. What are the "in" colors now?'

'It just depends,' Caroline replied. 'What type of room are you dealing with?'

'Bedroom, hallway, bathroom,' Rachel listed. 'Basically, the whole house.'

'We're starting with bedrooms, though,' Nick added.

Caroline snapped her fingers. 'You're working on the old Boyd mansion, aren't you?'

Rachel exchanged a glance with Nick. 'Why, yes. We are.'

'That's such a cool house,' Caroline gushed. 'We talked a lot about it in my art classes. Did you know they brought in a famous architect to design it?' Her brow furrowed. 'I can't remember who it was, but he was well known in his day.'

'I didn't know that,' Rachel said.

'Did you find the hidden treasure yet?' Caroline asked.

Nick interrupted. 'It's only an urban legend.'

The teenager's sunny expression dimmed. 'It's such a romantic story. Are you sure it isn't true?'

'Romantic?' Rachel asked. She hadn't heard anything about romance associated with the house.

'Oh, yes. We talked about it in history class,' Caroline assured them. 'Apparently one of the girls who lived in the house was going to marry a young man, but he went off to fight for the South. They were both quite wealthy and she hid her nest egg in the house for when he returned. Unfortunately, he died in one of the last Civil War battles.'

'And she died of a broken heart,' Nick finished.

'You *have* heard this story,' she exclaimed.

'No, I just guessed at how it ended,' he answered. 'Like I said, it's a basic, run-of-the-mill myth. Every town in America probably has one just like it.'

'It's still a nice story,' Caroline insisted. 'Anyway, the books you're looking for are over here.' She skirted her counter to lead them toward the shelves. 'It's hard to say which color is the most popular because I've ordered everything from pastels to the red flocked designs that were all the rage ages ago. I will say, though, that the bolder colors are making a comeback—moss green, navy blue, brown. The best thing to do is look through what's available and choose whatever catches your eye.'

Rachel smiled at her. 'Thanks.'

'Maybe when you're done, you'll give tours to the public.'

Caroline's hopeful note caused Rachel to agree. 'We'll have an open house and you're invited.'

As soon as Caroline left, Nick nudged Rachel. 'See? She said dark bold colors are the latest thing.'

'She also said that pastels were still popular,' Rachel reminded him. 'Why don't you pick out your four books and I'll pick out mine?'

Before long, they were on their way home with the bound samples in the trunk of Nick's car.

'We should mark the patterns we like in our books and then swap,' Rachel suggested.

'I'd rather study them together,' he said. 'Although I'd like your opinion of the jungle print I saw.'

'Jungle print? In a bedroom?'

'Sure. It makes sense.'

'How?'

He grinned. 'That's the room where all those animal instincts take over. You know, lions and tigers and—'

'Cavemen?' Rachel asked.

He laughed. 'You don't find it appealing to be dragged into a virile fellow's lair?'

Rachel giggled. 'Quite the courtship ritual. You *would* think of that.'

'Someone has to. After all—' His pager went off and he didn't finish his sentence as he read the display. 'I need a phone.'

'Are you on call?'

'Just for tonight,' he said. 'It's Mason's weekend, but he couldn't cover this evening, so I said I would.'

Fifteen minutes later, after he'd carried the books into the house and dialed the ER, he left. 'If you're still awake when I get home, I'll swing by for a late night snack. Do you have any of your grandma's gingerbread left?'

'Some,' she said. 'Didn't she bring you cookies yesterday?'

'Yeah, but they're gone.' His grin was sheepish. 'I couldn't help myself.'

'You ate two dozen cookies in one day?'

'Hey, I'm a growing boy,' he said, using the same excuse he'd used when they'd been kids.

'Yeah,' she teased back. 'Out, not up. Don't worry, I'll save you some of mine.'

'I'll be back,' he promised.

The sun was on its downward slope and as soon as it sank behind the tops of the trees, night fell in earnest. Rachel took advantage of Nick's absence to initiate the genuine reproduction antique fiberglass bathtub the plumber had installed the day before. As thrilled as she was to have her own bathroom again, she missed seeing Nick's tooth-brush in the holder and smelling his aftershave.

At ten, she decided to watch the news. After the ten-fifteen weather report, she daydreamed about the dress she intended to buy.

She couldn't recall being this excited about going out with anyone before. Even her first date with Charles couldn't compare. Then again, his kisses didn't either. While they weren't unpleasant, she didn't experience the same knee-tingling, take-your-breath-away emotion.

The lack wasn't particularly a minus, she told herself. She liked and respected Charles and the fact that they got along well made for a lasting relationship. Sparks of the intimate kind were highly overrated and, like all fires, they gradually burned themselves out.

Nick provided the perfect example. He was like a piece of flint. One look from him and the woman in question lit up like the Plaza in Kansas City on Christmas Eve. No doubt he created enough sparks to start a forest fire with each woman he took out, but obviously those little sparks never found enough kindling to keep the blaze going. No, Charles might not have the same flash as Nick and he certainly wasn't as good a kisser, but he was…

Her mind went blank. She couldn't think of the right adjective to describe Charles. Darn Nick for making her focus on Charles's faults instead of his attributes. Darn him for making her realize what she was missing.

And darn him for making her wish for a love that exploded with enough passion to send the world off its axis.

Nick trudged up the steps to his apartment at eleven-thirty and tossed his car keys onto the coffee-table. He hated coming home to an empty house when he was tired and his spirits were low. For the past several hours, he and Dylan had done all they could to diagnose and then stabilize his patient, but nothing had worked. Feeling the need for a cleansing shower, he headed for his bathroom.

Rachel had already cleared out her toiletries, which wasn't surprising since she now had a new tub to enjoy. After only one day, he missed the familiar fragrance of her shampoo and the clutter of lotions on the sink. Somehow those few bottles had made his place seem less lonely.

Suddenly, he couldn't wait to see her, even if it was almost midnight. Seven minutes later, his hair still wet, he strode across the yard, pleased to see the lights in her house glowing brightly.

He knocked first then, without waiting for her reply, he walked in. He followed the sound of low voices to her bedroom and found the television running. Rachel, however, lay on her bed fast asleep, her bare legs and arms sprawled in abandon.

Much as he wanted to talk, he couldn't force himself to wake her. She'd worked hard this past week. From dawn until late at night, she'd attacked the house's flaws with single-minded determination until they no longer existed. Perhaps she'd perform the same miracle with her private demons.

He found the remote control peeking out from underneath her pillow. After carefully sliding it free, he clicked the 'off' button and silence fell. He knew he should leave, but he couldn't. Instead, he drank in the view, unable to tear his gaze off the gentle rise and fall of her breasts, the fluttering of her eyelids as if she were viewing a movie and the smile gently curling her lips.

He remembered her passion and, illogically, he wanted to punch Chuckie in the nose for disappointing her. She'd never admit to it, but he'd heard the sound in her voice. Charlie clearly didn't realize the prize within his grasp.

Although he hadn't met the man, Nick wondered why Rachel was so willing to settle for someone who assigned more importance to computer interfaces than to her. She deserved a man who thought the sun, moon and stars rose in her and who couldn't get through each day without seeing the smile on her face. She deserved a man who supported her, who listened to her and who loved her. From the little he knew about Charles, Nick was sure about one thing. Charles wasn't the man for his Rachel and if Nick played his cards right, she would realize it, too.

His Rachel. The thought was bitter-sweet. He had no more claim to her than…Dylan had, but he still considered her as his. His friend. His confidante.

To his dismay, she was spoken for…almost. He wasn't about to do more than kiss her as long as Charlie hung on the fringes of her life, but as soon as he was out of the picture he wouldn't let Rachel slip through *his* hands.

Leaning down, he brushed a kiss on her forehead. 'Sweet dreams, Rach.' He clicked off the bedside lamp and left her room. As he walked through the kitchen to the back door, he noticed her Porky-the-Pig cookie jar on the table. On impulse, he raised the lid and grabbed four gingerbread cookies out of the six remaining.

As consolation, food was cold comfort compared to Rachel's warm embrace. For the time being, however, it would have to do.

At seven o'clock, Rachel glanced at herself in the upstairs bathroom mirror, wishing it were full length so she could check herself from head to toe. She'd simply have to rely on Nick's response once he saw her in the perfect little number she'd found.

'Little' was the operative word. Her gown was a sleeveless black sheath made out of some sort of silky fabric that clung to her like a second skin. Her grandmother would have considered the scoop neckline and mid-thigh hem daring, but Rachel felt adventuresome this evening. The moment she'd been waiting for was finally coming to pass— she would be on a date with Nick Sheridan. Just the two of them. In public. Who said that dreams never came true?

Speaking of Nick, she hadn't seen him all day. He'd come by last night—at least, she assumed he'd been the one who'd shut off her television and the lights, and helped himself to the cookies in her cookie jar. Obviously his patient had been more critical than he'd thought.

In any event, she'd flipped through the wallpaper samples all morning and had spent the afternoon shopping. As she eyed as much of the dress as she could see in the small mirror, she considered it had been a successful expedition.

The doorbell rang, and she hurried downstairs in her high heels, flattered by Nick's show of courtesy when he could have walked in, unannounced.

Breathless from her haste, she flung open the door. Nick stood on the porch, looking quite dashing in his suit and tie. 'Hi,' she said.

Nick whistled. 'Sufferin' catfish, Rachel! I'd better bring my whip and chair along.'

His masculine admiration sent her spirits soaring. 'What are you talking about?'

'I'll be fighting off the other men all night long.'

Rachel grabbed his arm and pulled him inside. 'I'm flattered you think so.'

He shook his head. 'I don't think, I *know*.'

Happiness unfolded inside her like a rose in bloom. Who said that the clothes didn't make the man...or woman? Right now, between the dress and his praise, she couldn't have been more thrilled if she'd won a million dollars.

'Our reservations are for eight,' he said, 'so, if you're ready, your chariot awaits.'

'Let me get my bag,' she said. Minutes later, her small clutch purse in hand, she allowed him to escort her outside to his waiting vehicle. She stopped short as she saw a sporty Corvette parked at the curb instead of his ten-year-old Pontiac. 'Is that yours?' she asked.

'Only for the evening.' He urged her forward with his hand resting on the base of her spine. 'Dylan let me borrow it.'

'Wow! I'm impressed,' she said, carefully sliding into the front seat. 'What did you have to promise him?'

'My firstborn,' he answered promptly. 'Or dinner when we finish the house. Whichever comes first.'

She laughed. 'I hope our project doesn't last that long. I don't think I could survive. People who do this for a living have earned my utmost respect.'

'Shall I assume you don't intend to start your own ''Rachel's Renovations'' business?'

'I don't think so. Ask me again, though, when I'm done. I may change my mind.' Although she didn't say so, she did miss the hustle and bustle of the hospital on occasion. Perhaps she could move into a teaching position instead of working in ER or on the floor.

The thirty-minute drive to Joplin passed swiftly, and when they arrived at their destination Rachel couldn't believe how the owner had transformed a run-down, weed-infested swimming pool into a beautiful villa.

Although she hadn't tasted Greek cuisine before, she discovered that she truly enjoyed the unusual flavors. Between the good food, the restaurant's ambience and the intimate table for two set in a cozy corner, she didn't know when she'd experienced a more perfect evening and she told Nick so.

'Now, aren't you glad you came?' Nick asked.

'Absolutely.'

After they'd eaten, they walked through the garden with its bushes, fountains and Greek urns. Later, they lingered near one of the Greek columns that was part of the huge gazebo and enjoyed the evening air.

'Someone turned off my lights last night,' she said, threading her arm through his. 'I assume that was you?'

'You really should lock your doors at night. I walked right in.'

'I didn't think you'd be gone long.'

'Even so,' he scolded. 'Don't do it again. I know how to knock and if it's necessary, I'll use my key.'

'Yes, sir,' she said in mock obedience. 'You never told me how your case went.'

He shrugged. 'Not so well.'

Rachel gripped his arm tighter. 'I'm sorry to hear it. What happened?'

'A sixty-five-year-old man came in with his wife. He complained of chest pain and we did the usual. His ECG showed some arrhythmia, but nothing out of the ordinary. We'd almost decided that he had an acute case of indigestion, but before we could send him home he arrested.'

'Good thing he was already in ER.'

'You would have thought so, but it didn't matter. After he coded we tried everything, but we couldn't bring him back. The pathologist did a post-mortem this morning at the family's request. A heart valve literally exploded. There was nothing we could have done.'

'I wish you would have woken me when you came in. We could have talked.'

He smiled. 'You looked too peaceful. Not only that, but I could filch as many cookies as I wanted without you noticing.'

The gloomy mood lifted. 'I saw this morning how you helped yourself.'

'I left you a couple,' he protested.

'Gee, thanks.'

'You should thank me,' he said. 'If I hadn't taken as many as I did, you wouldn't look as great in that dress as you do.'

'Then you really like it?'

'Honey,' he drawled, 'the only way I'd like it any better would be if it slid off your body and landed at your feet.'

Rachel's face warmed, although she hoped he wouldn't see her flushed skin in the growing twilight.

'Has Chauncey seen you in that?'

'No, *Charles* hasn't,' she said. 'I just bought it this afternoon.'

'I didn't think he had.'

She glanced up at him. 'What makes you say that?'

'Because I can't imagine how he'd let you wear it for anyone but him. I know I wouldn't.'

Rachel fell silent as she fingered the strand of pearls she'd received from her grandparents as a graduation present. It seemed perfidious to discuss how Charles rarely commented on what she was wearing. The few times he had, he'd used words like 'nice' or 'cute'. Sometimes, like right now, she wanted to hear words like 'knock-out' and 'gorgeous'.

'He doesn't pay attention to outward appearances,' she said instead.

'Too bad. He's missing out on a lot. Maybe you'll get an opportunity to wear it for him.'

'Maybe,' she said, although she doubted it. She had bought this dress with Nick in mind. She couldn't wear it for anyone else.

'I suppose we should head for home,' he said.

'It's getting late,' she agreed. 'Tomorrow will be here before we know it.'

'What *are* we doing tomorrow?'

'Choosing wallpaper, remember? I'll expect to see you promptly at one.'

'Don't you owe me a dinner?' he asked.

'I paid you back last week.'

'And I've provided two meals since then.'

She gave him a fake long-suffering sigh. 'All right. Come over at noon. My food won't compare to tonight's, though.'

'Don't worry. I can eat whatever you set in front of me.' He patted his stomach. 'Sheridans are tough.'

She giggled. 'OK, Dr Tough Guy. Let's go home.'

Later, as he deposited her on her front porch, she heard the distinct sound of wood cracking. 'I've just moved the steps higher on our priority list,' he said. 'All we need is for the mailman to fall through and break his leg.'

'Fine by me. Don't forget the squeaky boards upstairs.'

'I won't.' Nick unlocked the front door, flicked the light

switch, then blocked her from entering. 'Thanks for a great evening.'

'Thank you,' she said. 'I can't remember when I've enjoyed myself this much.' Although she didn't want him to leave, she also knew that inviting him in wouldn't be fair to either Charles or Nick.

'Me neither.' He bent his head and kissed her.

If she'd thought that the fireworks she'd seen during their first kiss had been a fluke, this one drove those notions right out of her head. The feel of his lips against hers produced the same heady sensations as before, and she was dimly aware of his arms encircling her. It was like the Fourth of July and Christmas all rolled into one.

Sooner than she wished, he released her. 'Sleep well.'

She could hardly force enough air through her lungs to speak. When she did, the sound came out as a whisper. 'You, too.'

Rachel walked inside and shot the deadbolt home automatically. It should be illegal for one man's kisses to be so potent. If he kissed every woman he'd taken out like he kissed her, how had he escaped the matrimonial knot?

She headed for her room and sat on the edge of the bed, unable to summon enough energy to change her clothes. Although she'd dreamed of sharing an evening like this with Nick, it had only created a moral dilemma for her. What would she do about Charles?

The answer was obvious. She might like Charles, and even love him for the nice man he was, but she wasn't *in love* with him. She didn't know what, if anything, would develop between herself and Nick, or if even what she felt for him was the love she saw between her grandparents and wanted for herself, but she'd never know for certain if she didn't cut her ties to Charles.

His inability to visit this weekend may have been a blessing in disguise.

Coming to that conclusion, she focused on her surroundings and heard footsteps. Thinking Nick had returned, she re-entered the kitchen. It was empty, but she could swear she wasn't alone.

The floorboards overhead creaked in their familiar fashion, and she wondered why Nick had gone upstairs. Curious, she hurried toward the staircase and was nearly run over near the front door.

Surprised, she squealed. Then, after realizing a split second later that the person who'd darted down the stairs garbed in black from head to toe wasn't Nick, she drew a deep breath and screamed.

Time passed in slow motion as she saw the intruder's uplifted arm and a glint of silver before shooting pain radiated through her skull. Her vision blurred and her world turned gray as the force of his blow drove her against the wall.

She slid to the floor, fighting the fog clouding her brain. Nick. She had to call Nick. Clinging to that thought, she nearly wept as her attempts to stand failed and the room whirled around her. Finally, unable to chase away the growing darkness, she gave up, mumbling his name.

CHAPTER SEVEN

NICK pulled Dylan's Corvette into the driveway and got out to open the garage doors. Not sure of how the evening would progress, he'd arranged to swap the other physician's car for his the next morning when he went to the hospital to make his rounds. Dylan, of course, had smirked and commented on how he hoped to see Nick before noon. While spending the night with Rachel was part of Nick's fantasy as well, his personal scruples wouldn't allow him to encroach upon Charles' territory to that degree.

He reached up to lower the garage door, but his internal warning system stopped him. He listened, expecting to hear the usual background noise of crickets and the neighborhood owl. Instead, an ominous silence filled the night air.

The hair on the back of his neck seemed to stand on end. A second later, he heard a muffled scream.

Rachel, he thought as he sprang into action. He sprinted across the yard, praying that the lights blazing in her house indicated all was well. He hoped there was a logical explanation—a television program, perhaps—but his instincts warned otherwise.

Nick bounded up the five back-door steps and reached for the doorknob, cursing as it refused to budge under his hard twist. He reached into his pocket and pulled out Dylan's keys instead of his own. Realizing that Rachel's key hung on the ring in Dylan's possession, he muttered several more choice words.

Without hesitation, he dashed to the front porch. His dread grew as the door she'd closed a short time ago now stood ajar. He rushed in, only to stop short as he saw her lying in the corner across from the staircase.

Tamping down his fear, he crouched beside her and pressed on her carotid. The tell-tale thump underneath his fingers registered and his shoulders drooped in pure relief.

The most obvious problem was the blood running down her face. The cut near her hairline was deep and would need stitches. The goose egg at the back of her head, however, worried him, and he imagined medical problems ranging from subdural hematomas to concussions.

'Rachel,' he urged aloud. 'Can you hear me?'

Her eyelids fluttered. 'What…?'

Heartened by her response, he commanded, 'Rachel? Open your eyes.'

While she struggled to comply, he quickly ran his hands over her body, pleased that she'd suffered no apparent broken bones or other injuries. However, he knew that he wouldn't feel totally certain of her condition until he hauled her to the hospital and checked her out from head to toe.

'Come on, honey,' he coaxed. 'You can do it. Talk to me.'

Her eyes fluttered open and for the first time since he'd heard the scream he was able to think positively. 'What…happened?' she asked.

'You tell me,' he said.

She winced as she touched her forehead. 'Give me a minute.'

Nick moved her hand. 'Don't touch,' he ordered gently. 'I'm going to get a towel. Just relax.'

He found one in the kitchen and pressed it to her open wound. 'Do you hurt anyplace else?'

'Other than my head?' She closed her eyes as if to concentrate. 'My shoulder.'

He gave special attention to her shoulder, carefully feeling the bone alignment. 'Nothing seems broken, but we'll know after an X-ray. I'm calling an ambulance.'

'Don't be ridiculous,' she said. 'It's just a cut. Let me up.'

'A cut that needs stitches,' he corrected, keeping his hand

on her collarbone so she couldn't rise. 'Don't forget the bump on the back of your head and the ache in your shoulder. You're going to the hospital, so just lie there.'

She obeyed, which in Nick's opinion was almost surprising. Yet if she suspected his plans to keep her in hospital overnight, she'd summon the energy to fight him tooth and nail.

'Any nausea, double vision?'

'Some.'

He stood. 'I'll phone 911 and—'

'No ambulance.'

He stopped in mid-stride. 'If you think for one minute that I'm not going to have Dylan check you out, you'd better think again.'

Rachel covered her eyes with her arm. 'Don't yell.'

He lowered his voice. 'I'm not yelling. All I'm saying is—'

'I'm not arguing about going to the ER,' she interrupted. 'From the way my head is pounding, I'd like to know if my brain is trying to leak out.'

Her attempt to make a joke was encouraging. Although it eased his mind that she wouldn't fade before his eyes, he couldn't fully understand the reasons for her objection. 'Then what's the problem?'

'I won't go in an ambulance.'

'Aren't you taking your fear a little too far?'

'Oh, I'm not afraid of the ride,' she said matter-of-factly. 'I just know how my grandparents think. They're going to hear what happened—it's inevitable in a town this size— and if they learn how I went to the hospital in an ambulance, they're going to imagine the worst. If we drive in your car, they won't worry as much.'

'Your grandparents will worry, regardless,' he said. 'Do you remember what happened?'

'A little,' she admitted. 'I walked inside, locked the front door and went to my room. I was about to undress when I heard a noise. I thought you might have come back so I went to check, but the room was empty.'

Hindsight being twenty-twenty, he already knew the next part of her story but asked anyway. 'Then what?'

'I started toward the living room, thinking that you were coming in. When I heard the floorboards creak, I couldn't imagine what you were doing on the second floor.'

'That was a crazy assumption to make,' he said, unable to contain himself. 'Why would I go up there if you were down here?'

'That's what I couldn't understand,' she retorted. 'I never dreamed someone other than you would be roaming around my house, uninvited. After all, this is Hooper, not Joplin or Springfield.'

'Didn't I tell you—'

Rachel held up her hands. 'Spare me the lecture, please. Believe me, next time I'll hide under the bed until it's safe. Anyway, I went to the living room and ran into someone. I remember realizing it wasn't you but in the next instant he hit me. My head seemed to explode and I went sailing.' She wriggled her arm. 'My shoulder must have hit the wall.'

'You could have been killed,' he said, relying on anger as an outlet for his fear.

'I wasn't. So no ambulance.'

Her concern for her grandparents, in spite of her own injury, touched him. 'It's noble of you to be worried about your grandparents' reaction, but there are times when you have to think of yourself.'

Her jaw visibly squared. 'If you call the paramedics, I won't go. I'm conscious, so I can refuse and no one can force me.'

Stubborn woman, Nick thought. 'Fine. I'll take you myself, but they *are* coming.'

'Why?'

'Because I want you in a neck brace and unless you have one lying around the house, we'll need theirs.'

'My neck doesn't hurt,' she said. 'Only my head, so don't waste their time. I mean it, Nick.'

'I'm calling the shots,' he said. 'I'm also notifying the police and, for your information, that's not negotiable either.'

The stiff set to her body disappeared and she sounded weary. 'Suit yourself.'

He strode into the kitchen, made his call and soon returned. 'Now we wait,' he said.

'Goody.'

Her sarcasm made him smile. The attack hadn't affected her sense of humor. 'I'm doing this for your health.'

She sighed. 'I know. I don't have to like it, though. I hate being a patient.'

'Sometimes we don't have a choice,' he said, knowing how difficult it was for her. She'd never liked appearing weak. 'I'll bring the car around as soon as the EMTs arrive.'

A slight grin teased the corners of her mouth. 'Why wait? I'm not moving from my spot. The sooner we leave, the sooner you can bring me back.'

Although he knew that wouldn't be the case, he chose not to begin that particular battle just yet. Instead, he said, 'Yeah, but I'd rather not leave you alone right now.'

'I doubt if he'll be back,' she said.

'Probably not, but indulge me.' Nick couldn't stand the idea of her lying in an empty house, unattended. It would be tough enough to leave her in the care of the EMTs for the few minutes it would take him to return with Dylan's Corvette.

She didn't answer, then whispered as she closed her eyes, 'Thanks.'

Before long, the emergency vehicles arrived with their lights flashing and sirens blaring. He ushered them in, explained the situation to the EMTs, then rushed to the garage. By the time he returned, they'd finished their preliminary assessments and Rachel was wearing a brace to support her neck. Although they, too, tried to encourage her to go with them, she refused.

'Nick's a doctor,' she told them. 'I'm in good hands.'

Her endorsement made Nick's heart swell with pride and he became even more determined to look after her. Finally, after accepting Nick's reassurances that he would personally see she got to the hospital, the EMTs left.

At that point, Officers Hawver and Marlow took charge. They both listened to Rachel's story although Hawver, the older and obviously more experienced member of the pair, jotted notes in his little black book. As she concluded, he turned to Nick. 'Did you see anyone leave the house?'

Nick shook his head.

Hawver flipped the pad closed and placed it in his left breast pocket. 'We'll take a look around.'

'While you do, I'm taking her to the hospital.'

'OK. We'll be in touch.' Hawver began his sweep of the house to find a point of entry while Marlow left, presumably to retrieve his fingerprinting kit.

'Do you think they'll find anything about my mystery guest?' Rachel asked, walking tentatively in spite of Nick's hand on her forearm. Nick was sure that each step must have sent fresh spasms of pain through her head and he intended to make sure she didn't lose her balance.

'Probably,' he said. 'The question is, will their results be of value? Between you, me, your grandparents and everyone else who's ever been in this house, it will be more a case of who *hasn't* touched the door than who has.'

'I guess you're right.' She hesitated at the top of the porch stairs. Without giving her a chance to argue, he swung her into his arms and carried her down the steps, carefully avoiding the weakened spots.

'What are you doing?' she asked, resting her head against his neck.

'What does it feel like?' he countered.

She made a little noise in her throat—one of those

breathy sounds that reminded him of her response to his kisses. 'I'm too heavy.'

'You're just right,' he said, not unhappy to have her in his arms as he strode down the sidewalk to the waiting car. 'I'm going to set you down while I open the door.'

'OK.'

Within minutes, he'd buckled her into her seat and they were on their way. Nick repeated the process in the ER driveway, carrying her inside instead of asking for a wheelchair. If anyone thought it strange to see one of their physicians with a patient in his arms, no one said a word.

'Which bed is available?' he asked the nurse on duty who met him near the automatic doors.

'Trauma two,' was her reply.

He strode toward the room in question and placed Rachel gently on the mattress. 'Possible skull fracture,' he said as Dylan poked his head through the curtains. 'I want a CT scan and routine films of her right shoulder and C-spine.'

'You got 'em,' he said. 'For the record, am I the doctor on this case or are you?'

Rachel answered. 'You are.'

'But I'm the consultant,' Nick added.

At Dylan's raised eyebrow, Nick squared his shoulders and mentally dared him to comment. Instead, his colleague simply nodded. 'Want to tell me what happened?' He paused to glance at Nick. 'My car isn't involved, is it?'

'Your toy is safe,' Nick told him. 'Rachel surprised a burglar.'

Dylan probed the cut on her forehead. 'You're not supposed to do that, Rachel,' he said mildly.

'Yes, I know,' she answered wryly.

'You'll need several stitches,' he commented.

'Can't you just glue the edges together?'

'I could, but I need the sewing practice.' Dylan's fingers moved to the knot at the back of her head.

'Ouch!' Rachel exclaimed.

'That's quite a bump you have.'

'No kidding.'

Dylan shone his penlight in her eyes, then held up two fingers. 'How many fingers do you see?'

Rachel squinted. 'Four. I think.'

'She was unconscious for several minutes,' Nick supplied.

'Nausea?' Dylan asked.

'Some.' Rachel and Nick spoke together and Dylan smiled. 'At least you two agree.'

'Only on rare occasions,' Rachel said. 'What's your prognosis? Take two aspirin and call you in the morning?'

'First, let's see what our handy-dandy X-rays show,' Dylan quipped as he unwound his stethoscope to listen to her heart and lungs. 'No sense in letting our staff twiddle their thumbs tonight. I'll also prescribe a pain reliever for your head. It hurts, I imagine.'

She rubbed her temples. '"Hurts" is an understatement. It's more like a herd of cattle stampeding in my skull.'

Dylan motioned to the nurse and she soon brought a small cup of water and two little white pills. 'This will take the edge off,' Dylan told Rachel as she swallowed them. 'But as you know, they're non-narcotic. We don't want you sleeping yet.'

The radiology technician appeared in the doorway and Dylan waved her through, repeating the orders Nick had already given. As soon as she'd wheeled Rachel away, Nick spoke to Dylan.

'I want her admitted.'

Dylan nodded. 'Absolutely. If she lost consciousness for several minutes, she needs close observation.'

'Rachel won't want to stay.'

'Who does?' Dylan asked. 'I'm guessing that when she gets back from Radiology, she'll be more than ready to try our accommodations.'

'Be prepared for a fight if she's not.'

By the time she returned from her X-rays and Dylan had sutured her forehead, Rachel appeared to have as much stamina as a cooked noodle and the color of her face matched the white sheets. Nick hovered nearby, holding her hand because he couldn't seem to let it go. Next time, he assured himself, he would walk through the house with her before he left her alone.

'What's the verdict?' she asked.

'The good news is there are no signs of a subdural hematoma or a skull fracture,' Dylan said. 'Your C-spine is A-OK, and your shoulder is only bruised.'

'Then what's the bad news?' she asked.

Dylan gave Nick a sidelong glance. 'You have a concussion.'

She dismissed his diagnosis with a wave of her free hand. 'Is that all?'

'It's serious enough to earn you a bed upstairs.'

Her jaw dropped for a second. 'You just said everything was fine,' she accused, glancing back and forth between the two men.

'You don't have any broken bones,' Dylan corrected. 'According to Nick, you lost consciousness for several minutes. I can't let you go home.'

Rachel glared at Nick, pulling her hand free from his. 'You put him up to this, didn't you?'

'Now, Rachel,' Nick soothed. 'He's only doing his job.'

'I know the drill. Someone will wake me every hour and ask me who the President of the United States is or today's date. I can do that at home.'

'But who will ask those questions?' Nick asked, relying on what he hoped would be his trump card. 'Shall I get your grandmother out of bed so she can babysit you?'

She frowned, apparently considering the option and not liking it. 'No.'

'It's only overnight,' Dylan soothed. 'Less than that, in fact, since it's nearly two a.m.'

Nick sensed that she was close to giving in. 'What time can I leave?' she asked.

Dylan shoved his hands in his lab coat pockets. 'Why don't we talk about this after you wake up?'

'I don't have much choice, do I?'

'Not really,' he said cheerfully.

Before he could say more, the nurse poked her head into the cubicle. 'I need you in room five, Doctor.'

'I'll be right there.' He winked at Rachel. 'If you'll excuse me, I have *real* patients to see.'

Soon Nick was left alone with Rachel. 'They're going to admit you to room 307. I'm—'

'You had this planned all along, didn't you?' she asked.

'The established protocol requires hospital observation in cases like yours,' he hedged. 'Dylan might act like he doesn't have a serious bone in his body, but when it comes to medicine, he goes strictly by the book.'

'Great,' she said glumly.

He grinned. 'But if he wasn't going to admit you, I intended to pull rank as your consulting physician. And if you weren't going to listen, I was going to call on the big guns—your grandparents.'

'I give up. I should be angry with you, you know,' she said, stifling a yawn. 'And I will be just as soon as my headache goes away.'

'I'm looking forward to it. Now, I'm going to move Dylan's car before it gets towed for blocking the ambulance entrance. If you're not here when I get back, I'll find you.'

'Room 307.'

'Hey, you're pretty sharp.'

'Then I can go home?'

'Later,' he said. Unable to stop himself and not caring if he had an audience, he leaned over and kissed her mouth. 'Behave yourself while I'm gone.'

She smiled. 'Speak for yourself.'

'Hey,' he said, pretending affront. 'I always behave.' Even when I don't want to, he thought to himself. 'I'll see you in a few minutes.'

'Aren't you going home?'

'After you're settled.'

She yawned again. 'You're really a very nice guy. Do you know that?'

'Of course. All you had to do was ask me.' In his heart, though, he hoped she'd feel the same once she learned about the phone call he intended to make first thing in the morning.

Rachel awoke to find Nick dozing in the chair beside her bed, his face showing a trace of dark stubble under the faint illumination of the nightlight. She glanced at the wall clock and gasped aloud.

Nick instantly rose half out of his chair. 'What's wrong?'

'It's ten o'clock,' she said inanely, pressing the button to raise the head of the bed to a sitting position. 'At night.'

He settled back down, blinking like an owl. 'Yeah. So?'

'I slept the entire day away?'

'More or less. How are you feeling?'

She took stock of her aches and pains. None were too bad, which was amazing when she considered how she'd felt. 'I'm fine. The headache's almost gone.'

'Good.'

'Were you here the whole time?'

He shrugged. 'Off and on.'

'You must have been here more ''on'' than ''off'' because you woke me to ask those ridiculous questions. Which, now that I think about it, you could have done at my house.'

Nick shrugged. 'I wanted you where we could do something if your condition changed.' He paused. 'I thought my questions were quite intelligent.'

'The day of the week and the name of our governor were good,' she admitted. 'But the name of my favorite teacher?'

He appeared affronted. 'I could have asked how much you weigh.'

'And I wouldn't have told you.'

'I don't know about that,' he said, shaking his head. 'You

were willing to promise anything if I would let you sleep. At five o'clock, you became quite crabby. If I recall, you even suggested where I could stuff my stethoscope.'

Heat flooded her face as her words drifted out of her memory. 'Sorry about that, but I prefer waking on my own.'

'I'll remember that.'

She was certain she heard a gentle caress in his voice and wondered what it would be like to open her eyes each morning to find him beside her. She'd rub her hands over his whiskered face, kiss him and— Instantly she put the brake on those thoughts and forced them in another direction.

'Didn't you go home?' she asked, noting he'd changed clothes from when she'd seen him last but they were still rumpled.

'About seven this morning. It's been a long day,' he said simply.

Rachel swung her legs over the edge of the bed, carefully arranging her hospital gown to cover herself. 'Well, you can go now and take me with you.'

'No can do.'

'Dylan said I could leave when I woke up. My eyes are open. See?' She batted her eyelashes.

'Be serious. It's past your bedtime. Dylan will release you in the morning.'

'But I don't want to stay until morning,' she argued. 'I'm not sleepy.'

'Now, Rachel,' he began.

'Fine. I'll sign myself out. AMA. Against medical advice.'

'How will you get home? I'm not going to drive you.'

'I'll call a taxi.'

'We have one taxi service in Hooper and they don't operate after nine p.m.'

'Then I'll walk.'

He rose. 'OK. Take a turn down the hallway with me. Then we'll see.'

'I need a robe.'

He approached with an extra hospital gown he'd taken off a pile on the counter. 'Hold out your arms,' he ordered. As soon as she'd slipped it on backwards, he helped her with her socks. 'All set?' he asked.

'Sure.'

His hand hovered near her arm as she came slowly to her feet. 'How are you doing?' he asked.

She felt a little woozy, but didn't mention it. He'd whisk her back to bed so fast her head would spin like a top, and at the moment it didn't need any extra help. 'Let's go.'

Gripping Nick's arm because it was comforting to draw on his strength, she slowly walked to the door then down the long hall before she pivoted to retrace her steps. Her bed looked more inviting once she returned, but it still wasn't the place she wanted to be.

'Are you sure you won't take me home?' she asked.

'Not unless you want to bunk with your grandparents. They were here most of the day, but they left when visiting hours ended.'

'How were they?'

'They handled the news well. Once I explained how you were sleeping because you were worn out and not because you were in a coma, they weren't as concerned.'

'I guess I can stay another night,' she said in her most long-suffering tone. Although she hated to admit defeat, the prospect of having her grandmother fuss over her gave her no other choice. 'You shouldn't have rushed me during our walk, though.'

'You set the pace, Rach,' he said. 'If we'd gone any slower, you would have taken root.'

'Very funny.' She sank onto the bed and gratefully accepted Nick's help to slide her legs under the blanket. 'By the way, have you heard from the police?'

'The person or persons involved pried open a window to get inside.'

'But what were they doing in my house? There's nothing of value. Most of the rooms are empty.'

'Their theory is that the guilty party was looking for the historic treasure associated with the house.'

Rachel frowned. 'How in the world can they tell?'

'Because of the holes he punched in the walls.'

'The ones I slaved over to get ready for new paper?' After scraping and sanding, she doubted if her knuckles would ever be the same.

He nodded, appearing as disgruntled as she felt. 'Yes.'

'Why those...rotten... I'd like to get my hands on this guy.'

Nick's gaze traveled to her forehead and his expression became grim. 'So would I.'

'I guess we're back to square one.'

'It's not as bad as you think. Repairing the damage shouldn't take too long and we can use the extra time to choose our paper pattern. By the way, I arranged for us to keep the books longer.'

She nodded, trying not to be discouraged by the setback and failing miserably.

'Because I don't want him or anyone else coming back,' Nick said, 'I'm also taking the story to the newspaper.'

'What good will that do? He's not going to respond to any appeal you might make.'

'I'm not making an appeal,' he told her. 'I want to debunk the myth.'

'I don't see—'

He patiently explained. 'If people read an article about the legend and learn how we've gone through every nook and cranny and haven't found any valuables, the treasure-hunters in town will leave us alone.'

'It's an idea, I suppose.'

'It's the *solution*,' he said firmly. 'The police even agree.'

'But every town needs a legend.'

'Not if it endangers your life,' he said. 'For Pete's sake, Rachel. If he'd hit you in the right spot, you'd be pushing up daisies.'

'Thanks for that mental picture,' she said dryly.

'I'm serious.'

One look at him convinced her of his sincerity. 'You were really worried, weren't you?'

'Damn right I was,' he said impatiently. 'You walk into a house and see a person you lo—a person you know lying on the floor with her face covered in blood. Don't tell me you wouldn't think the worst.'

She thought back to seeing Grace on the stretcher. She'd begged God, pleaded in every way she knew how to spare the lives of her friend and little Molly. Yes, she knew exactly how Nick had felt.

'OK. If you think the newspaper story is a good idea, go for it. Now, would you do me a favor?'

'What's that?'

She gazed at him fondly. 'Go home and sleep in your own bed. That chair can't be comfortable.'

'It's not,' he admitted.

'However,' she added, certain he would obey, 'I'll expect you here sharply at eight o'clock to drive me home.'

'How about noon?'

'Eight,' she commanded. 'And not one minute after.'

'All right, but on one condition. You're going to take things easy tomorrow. No physical labour of any kind. You won't budge anything heavier than a page in those wallpaper books.'

She would have promised him anything, but he didn't need to know that. 'It's a deal.'

He leaned over her to kiss her fully on the lips. A slow, lingering kiss. 'Goodnight, Rach.'

She could hardly find her breath as she stroked his cheek. 'Goodnight, Nick.'

At that moment, a red-haired nurse in her late forties,

LuAnn, appeared next to Rachel's bed, carrying an electronic thermometer. 'Are you still here?' she asked Nick.

'Not for long.' He waggled his fingers at Rachel, then disappeared.

LuAnn's question reinforced Rachel's suspicions, but she wanted them confirmed. 'Didn't Dr Sheridan leave at all today?'

LuAnn placed the probe in Rachel's ear. 'According to what I heard on my report, he's been here ever since you were admitted, except for about thirty minutes. I came on duty at two, and he hasn't left this room until now.'

'Really?'

LuAnn nodded. 'He wouldn't let the staff do anything for you either. Why, he even took your vital signs.' She winked. 'You've certainly set the tongues wagging. He seems more attentive to you than most. The ones who were hoping to catch his eye will have to wait several more weeks.'

Rachel refused to place too much credence on the nurse's observation. Just because he'd taken her to dinner and bestowed a few of his potent kisses on her, that didn't mean she'd become his current flavor of the month. 'Don't be silly. We're just friends—'

'Keep thinking that, honey,' LuAnn advised. 'It will save you a world of hurt.'

'Then he's left a trail of broken hearts?' Rachel knew the answer, but asked anyway.

'It's more a trail of disappointed ones. You see, he rarely goes out with the same woman more than a few times. Don't get me wrong. He's a great guy, but I get the impression he's only shopping around. When he finds the right one, he'll latch onto her.' Her gaze became speculative. 'Now that I think about it, it could be you.'

The possibility packed as much punch as the guy who'd creamed her with his wrench. For a frivolous moment, she let herself imagine it was true. The notion of winning

Nick's love was too big to comprehend, although if wishes were ever granted, that would be one of her dearest.

Yet her logic refused to let her dwell on such a fairy-tale because that was exactly how she'd describe LuAnn's story—as a fairy-tale. Nick had always seemed to gravitate toward tall, leggy, outgoing, cheerleader types, not quiet, studious women like herself. And as a highly successful physician, he certainly wouldn't choose a woman who toted a ton of professional baggage with her.

LuAnn blithely continued. 'I haven't known Dr Sheridan very long, but I've seen enough single men to know they prefer being the hunter and not the hunted. If the females around here would realize Dr Sheridan is no exception, they might have a chance.'

LuAnn definitely had a point. Nick attracted members of the opposite sex with seeming ease, but she couldn't recall him ever setting out to do so. 'My grandmother's favorite cliché is "The best things in life don't come easy."'

The other nurse agreed. 'Remember that if you expect Dr Sheridan to keep coming around.' She jotted her numbers on her notepad and gathered up her equipment. 'Sleep well.'

'Goodnight.' Unfortunately, LuAnn's conversation played over and over in Rachel's head. Her emotions swung back and forth like a pendulum as hope that Nick had been waiting for *her* his whole life competed with her logic.

Nick himself had admitted that one of his failures included a particular girl who hadn't succumbed to his charms. Perhaps Nick *was* holding out for the prize he had to win rather than the one simply handed to him. After all, he was an over-achiever and as such, if something wasn't worth working for, it wasn't worth attaining. The young lady he'd wanted and hadn't been able to catch was the one who'd played hard to get.

As for her being the so-called 'right' one, the idea was so remote it was ludicrous. Their chemistry might be pow-

erful and they might be comfortable enough to share secrets, but her idea of happily-ever-after didn't include a
constant battle of wills.

Having come to her conclusion, she gradually became
aware of a persistent patient bell dinging in the background.
After five more minutes, the bell's measured cadence became annoying.

Rachel wondered what had happened to LuAnn and the
rest of the staff. Thoroughly disgruntled, she crawled out
of bed and stood in the hallway outside her room. The
nurses' station was vacant, but the noise continued relent-
lessly.

The light above the door to nearby room 312 flashed, so
she ambled in that direction. No one had responded by the
time she got there, so she peered inside. A white-haired
lady sat in the bed, which had its head raised, and her face
reflected obvious pain.

Rachel once again glanced down the dimly lit hall, but
not a single soul was in sight. She didn't want to respond,
but she wouldn't sleep as long as the call bell rang. Neither
would she sleep if she didn't at least try to do what she
could to alleviate the woman's suffering. After taking a
bracing breath and berating herself for getting involved, she
padded inside.

CHAPTER EIGHT

RACHEL approached the bed. 'What's wrong?' she asked kindly.

The white-haired lady who was wearing a pink bed-jacket, cradled her right wrist and sniffed. 'I'll tell you what's wrong,' she began with a testy note in her voice. Suddenly she stopped her tirade as she eyed Rachel's hospital gown. 'You're not a nurse.'

'I am, but right now I'm a patient, too.' Rachel told her, using what she called her soothing-the-recalcitrant-patient tone. 'If you'll tell me the problem, I'll see what I can do.'

The lady stretched out her arm. 'I want this IV removed. It hurts terribly.'

Rachel took her hand and examined it. A dark bruise was spreading and the area around the needle was swollen and warm to the touch. The line had infiltrated and would have to be moved to another location.

'Your IV definitely needs to come out,' Rachel commented, trying to sound upbeat. 'The fluid is leaking into the tissue rather than going into your vein. It happens sometimes.'

'Can you help me?'

Rachel immediately checked the bag hanging from the pole, noting its contents of normal saline and an antibiotic. Shutting off the flow wouldn't create life-threatening problems although it would throw off the timing of the antibiotic administration. Still, it couldn't be helped. The patient wasn't benefiting if the solution didn't enter her circulatory system.

'I could,' she said, referring to changing the IV site. 'But I can't. I'm not on staff.'

The woman sniffed again. 'I've been ringing the bell and no one answers. If this is the sort of care one can expect

123

here, I'll certainly let the CEO know why I'm taking my medical business elsewhere.'

'I'll see if I can find someone,' Rachel promised. 'In the meantime, I've closed the line so the problem won't get worse.'

'Bless you, dear. What did you say your name was?'

Rachel wasn't sure she should give it, but she did.

'You're Hester's granddaughter, aren't you?'

'Yes, I am.'

'Good people, Hester and Wilbur.'

'Yes, they are.' Rachel edged toward the door. 'I'll find the nurse on duty.'

She sauntered down the hall, peeking into each room she passed. Everyone was either asleep or appeared to be resting quietly. That changed as soon as she reached the halfway mark. Even from this distance, she became aware of more activity than usual in the last room on the right.

Approaching cautiously so as not to interfere, Rachel stood in the hall at a point far enough to be out of the way and yet close enough to tell what was happening. The small private room was filled to bursting with equipment and personnel, but she only recognized Dylan and LuAnn among those surrounding the patient's bed. A crash cart stood nearby and she knew she'd walked into the middle of a code blue—a heart attack.

One woman stood off to the side with a notepad and was obviously acting as the official recorder. Because memories weren't always reliable after an emergency, her documentation of every therapeutic intervention and the patient's response was crucial.

From Rachel's vantage point, she caught a glimpse of the patient's exposed chest. Dylan grabbed a pair of cardiac paddles out of a nurse's hand and waited for her to squirt the conductive gel on the flat surfaces. He then placed one beneath the patient's clavicle, to the right of the upper end of his sternum, and pressed the other against the left wall of the chest, left of the cardiac apex.

Although Rachel wasn't close enough to see, she'd been

involved in enough similar situations to know that he'd pressed the 'charge' button and was waiting for the electric charge to build to the desired level.

'Clear,' he called out.

Everyone stood back. As Dylan depressed the 'discharge' button, the energy jolted the man's body. The monitor went from a straight line to blips that gradually settled into a regular rhythm.

'OK,' Dylan announced. 'Let's get him to ICU. I want the usual…'

Rachel blocked out his orders as she watched the staff's well-orchestrated movements. She hadn't really realized how much she missed the drama of those times they had cheated the Grim Reaper of another victim. Unfortunately, she wasn't convinced of her ability to still do so.

Several nurses guided the bed toward the door and Rachel stepped out of their path as they entered the hallway. Dylan followed but he paused when he caught sight of her.

'I'll meet you in the unit,' he told the team before he addressed Rachel. 'A little late to roam the halls, isn't it?'

'I couldn't sleep. One of the patients near me was having problems and I came to find LuAnn.' She motioned toward the nurse who was trying to restore order out of the chaos they had left behind.

'What sort of problem?' he asked.

'Her IV infiltrated.' She inclined her head in the direction of the disappearing group. 'How's the patient?'

'He converted fairly rapidly,' he said, using the terminology that referred to how quickly the man had responded to defibrillation. 'I'm hoping to stabilize him so we can have the folks in Joplin install a pacemaker.'

'I'm glad.'

He smiled. 'After all that excitement, don't you want to trade your putty knife for a stethoscope?'

'I'll think about it,' she said.

'Do that. Now, if you'll excuse me?' He loped down the hallway, disappearing around the corner leading to the elevators just as LuAnn came out of the room.

'Did you need something?' an extremely flushed LuAnn asked.

'The lady in 312 has an infiltrated IV. I shut it off, but she needs some attention.'

LuAnn groaned. 'I'll be there as soon as I can. It's going to be a while though.'

'Why don't I take out the IV?' Rachel offered. 'Then, when you have time, you can restart it.'

'Go ahead, but I'm not looking forward to poking her again. It took me for ever to find a vein on her last time, and she wasn't too happy with me by the time I'd finished.'

'Maybe someone else could try.'

'I'm the only nurse on this floor. I'll have to call the house supervisor, but she went to ICU with Mr Jones.'

'Sounds as if you don't have much choice.'

'I know.' LuAnn sighed. 'Mrs Parker is on a gentamicin drip, so if we don't get it running again, her whole schedule will be off kilter. Dr Rockhurst goes ballistic if his orders aren't followed to the letter.'

Because gentamicin was a powerful antibiotic, the blood levels had to be checked at various stages of the drug's administration in order to determine the peak and trough levels. If the trough or low levels were too low, the amount of antibiotic in the patient's bloodstream wasn't enough to counteract the infection. If the peak levels were too high, they would face the problem of drug toxicity. All in all, her treatment required close monitoring.

Unfortunately, Rachel couldn't provide LuAnn with any solutions save one, and since she wasn't on staff, offering to start the IV was asking for trouble. If something should happen...

'Anyway, thanks for telling me,' LuAnn said. 'And, please, tell Mrs Parker that someone will be there as soon as possible. If I'm lucky, it won't be me.'

Rachel returned her grin. 'I'll pass along the message.'

She retraced her earlier steps to Mrs Parker's room. 'Well?' the woman demanded.

'The nurse has been tied up with a patient at the other

end of the hall. She'll be here in a few minutes. In the meantime, I'm going to remove this so you'll feel more comfortable.'

Rachel found her supplies and soon disconnected Mrs Parker from her tubes. 'There you go,' she said. 'It shouldn't be much longer until the nurse comes in.'

'Won't you stay and visit?' Mrs Parker asked. 'It will help me pass the time. That is, if you're not too tired to talk to an old woman?'

Rachel ignored the faint throb in her head caused by bending over Mrs Parker's hand and sat in the nearby chair. 'I'd be happy to.'

'So explain why you're a nurse, but you're not working as one.'

Rachel smiled at the old lady's bluntness. 'I live in Wichita, but I came to Hooper for a while so I could help my grandparents with my Great-Aunt Matilda's house.'

'Ah, yes. The Boyd place. Then you don't intend to make your home here permanently?'

'I haven't made plans one way or another.'

'You're running away from something, aren't you?' Mrs Parker's brown eye color may have faded, but her gaze remained sharp.

'I'm on vacation,' Rachel corrected, although the older woman's observation was more on target than she might have wished.

'I didn't realize hospitals gave their employees such long holidays,' Mrs Parker said, her tone speculative.

Because Mrs Parker seemed the type of person who spent her time sticking her nose in other people's business, Rachel used a light-hearted tone to throw her off the scent. 'I needed a break.'

'Nursing can be rather demanding, I suppose,' she said idly.

Pictures of her most recent cases rolled through Rachel's mind. 'Yes, it is.'

'You've lost your sense of purpose. Your edge.'

Rachel froze as Mrs Parker homed in on her problem with amazing accuracy. 'How did you know?'

Mrs Parker's eyes sparkled with merriment. 'I've always prided myself on my intuition and my powers of observation. I may be old, my hair is gray and my teeth sit beside my bed, but I still have eyes and ears and I'm not afraid to use them.'

'Oh.'

'Don't worry, dear.' Mrs Parker patted Rachel's hand. 'We all lose things. Sooner or later, we usually find them.'

'But what if we don't?'

'Then maybe it was under our nose the entire time and we simply overlooked it. I can't begin to tell you how many times I thought I'd lost my glasses and then found them hiding in plain sight.' She cleared her throat. 'Enough of this depressing talk. What brings you here as a patient?'

Rachel fingered the bandage on her forehead as she tried to follow the abrupt change of subject. 'Someone was in my house and in his rush to leave I got in the way. The police think he was looking for the hidden treasure.'

Mrs Parker chortled. 'Anyone with any sense knows that story is a piece of fiction.'

'So I've heard.'

'And you don't think it's pure conjecture?'

Rachel smiled. 'I'm sure you're right, but it's fun to imagine otherwise. Everyone needs to believe in something.'

Mrs Parker's sharp-eyed gaze softened. 'You're absolutely correct. It's even more important that we believe in ourselves. It's so tragic when we don't. Wouldn't you agree?'

Before Rachel could answer, LuAnn and another woman in uniform walked in. 'I hear you've had some IV trouble, Mrs Parker,' she said.

'Yes, and I don't mind telling you that the service here is *abominable*. It's a sad day when another patient has to help you.' The sweet little old lady had transformed back into the haughty woman.

'I'm very sorry,' the supervisor, Norma Quill, said. 'But we're going to take care of it now.'

'I should say so,' Mrs Parker huffed. 'As a member of the Board of Directors, I intend to report my experience here to the appropriate people.'

Norma appeared undeterred by the threat. 'I hope you do. Maybe we'll be allowed to recruit more staff.'

Apparently Mrs Parker had expected the other nurse to bow and scrape because when she didn't, the wind blew out of Mrs Parker's proverbial sails. For the next several minutes, she pressed her lips together and didn't say a word except to ask Rachel to remain with her during the procedure.

Norma attempted to start a new line in Mrs Parker's other hand, but she failed twice as the older woman's spidery veins collapsed. To the patient's credit, she didn't utter a single complaint.

Norma sighed. 'I guess we'll need to call in one of the nurse-anesthetists. I'm not having any luck.'

'Humph,' Mrs Parker said. 'Why don't you let Rachel try?'

Three pairs of eyes fell on Rachel. 'I couldn't,' she said. 'I'm not on staff.'

'Nonsense,' Mrs Parker said. 'You're a nurse, so why make someone get out of bed if you can do the job?' Her eyes twinkled. 'I promise not to sue you or the hospital either.'

Rachel glanced at the fiftyish supervisor, hoping she would back her decision. Instead, Norma shrugged. 'If you want to, be my guest.'

At Rachel's hesitation, Mrs Parker continued. 'For land's sakes, girl. You can't do any worse and I would like to go to sleep before this night is completely over.'

'All right,' Rachel agreed. She quickly tied the tourniquet below Mrs Parker's left elbow, found a vein, inhaled a bracing breath and inserted a small-gauge needle. To her relief, the line filled with blood and soon the IV fluid was dripping as it should.

'Smooth as silk,' Mrs Parker announced.

'Pure luck.' Rachel rose. 'Now, if you don't mind, I'll see you all in the morning.'

Minutes later, she slipped between the hospital sheets and reflected on Mrs Parker's words of wisdom. What had she said? Something like, 'Sooner or later, we usually find the things we've lost.'

Perhaps that was true in some cases, but Rachel knew it didn't apply to her. She'd lost faith in herself and didn't have the courage to look for it.

'I have a surprise for you,' Nick said as he escorted Rachel across the yard to her back door.

'Another one?'

He appeared puzzled. '*Another* one. What do you mean?'

Rachel grinned at him. 'You were on time this morning.'

'I'm always on time,' he protested. 'Except when something else comes up.'

She laughed. 'Aren't we all? So what's my second surprise?'

Nick motioned her inside. 'You'll find out in a minute.'

Rachel walked into the kitchen. 'Where is it?'

He glanced around. 'Must be on the front porch.'

That explained why he'd taken a different route home and driven straight toward the garage. Curious, she hurried through the house, only to slow down as she approached the staircase and the scene of the crime.

As if Nick sensed her fear, he placed a comforting hand on her shoulder. 'Are you OK?'

She nodded, then continued through the door. 'I don't see any—'

The rest of her sentence remained unspoken as Rachel saw Charles leaning against a pillar, gazing at the young woman beside him in rapt adoration.

'Charles?' she asked, incredulous at both his presence and his display of devotion. He'd never stared at her like that during one of *their* conversations.

Charles jumped to attention. Although he smiled, a trace

of guilt appeared in his eyes and he rushed forward to grab her hand. 'Rachel! You're looking better than I'd expected.'

Rachel turned to Nick. 'This is my surprise?'

He appeared slightly less stunned than she felt. 'More or less.'

She pulled her thoughts together and remembered her manners. 'How nice of you to visit, Charles.' After a quick glance at the petite blonde who lingered in the background, she met Charles's gaze with a direct one of her own. 'Did you finish your project at the hospital?'

'No,' he said. 'But Nick called me yesterday and—'

Once again, she turned toward Nick. 'You did?'

'I thought he should know what happened,' he said simply.

His thoughtfulness brought tears to her eyes. 'Thanks.'

'You're very welcome.'

Rachel blinked away the gathering wetness and swallowed the lump in her throat. The bump on her head must have made her emotional if this small gesture nearly had her blubbering like a baby. She stepped past Charles and extended her hand to the blonde. 'We've never been introduced. I'm Rachel.'

'I'm Krissy,' the blonde said. 'Charlie and I, well, we—'

'We're working on the interface project together,' Charles inserted smoothly. 'Krissy deals with the instrument and I work on the computer hospital information system. We're pooling our knowledge and resources in order to make everything come together.'

From the conversation Rachel had interrupted, she suspected there was more 'coming together' than the mere transfer of data. The fact that her suspicions didn't cause any heart-wrenching emotion seemed to confirm what she'd suspected about her own feelings for Charles but had chosen to ignore.

'Why don't we all sit down and visit?' she said brightly. 'There's plenty of chairs to go around.'

'We can't stay long,' Charles began.

'Now, Charlie,' Krissy said, choosing a lawn chair next to Charles's. 'we have plenty of time.'

Rachel exchanged a glance with Nick, wondering if he'd caught the nickname Charles had suddenly acquired. Nick's wink and broad smile before he erased it from his mouth suggested that he, too, had noticed.

Nick smoothly started the conversation while Rachel listened, watched and generally felt as if she'd stumbled into an old episode of *The Twilight Zone*. As she compared the two men, Nick's dark complexion and his extroverted personality contrasted sharply with Charles's fairness and his quiet demeanor. At the same time, she couldn't help but notice how Charles's sidelong glances at Krissy held a tenderness that Rachel hadn't ever seen directed toward her.

Charles had never indicated that their relationship wasn't all that he wanted it to be, but the fact that he'd left his precious project—on a weekday, no less—to venture out of town with Krissy was significant. Obviously their separation had made him rethink what he wanted out of life in general and their relationship in particular, just as it had caused her to re-examine her priorities. She sensed that today's visit was more than just an opportunity for Charles to spread get-well wishes.

In that moment, she knew beyond all doubt that no matter how comfortable she was with Charles, how well they got along and how nice a person he was, Charles deserved to have someone who brought the sparkle to his eye. If Krissy was the one who turned Charles from a computer automaton into a lovesick man, Rachel couldn't stand in his way.

Krissy stood and asked with a giggle, 'Where's the little girls' room?'

Before Rachel could give directions, Nick rose. 'Come on. I'll take you to the carriage house apartment. The plumbing here has some problems.'

Rachel managed to keep her mouth from dropping open in surprise. They had just spent a small fortune for the plumber to lay new pipes and to install a beautiful new bathtub and toilet. There had better not be any problems or she wasn't paying the bill.

However, at Nick's raised eyebrow, she suddenly understood what he'd done. He'd given her time alone with Charles, and she was grateful.

As soon as Nick and Krissy had left, she smiled at the man who'd been a good friend, and who she hoped would remain so. 'Krissy seems like a nice girl.'

'Oh, she is.' Charles's face brightened and showed as much if not more animation than he exhibited when talking about his beloved computers. 'After Nick called, Krissy said she'd come with me so I wouldn't have to drive by myself.'

'Then you left this morning?'

'No, we got here late last night. The Horseshoe Inn isn't too bad a place to stay.'

Another telling point, she thought wryly. 'Charles, there's something—'

'Rachel, we need to—'

As they'd spoke at the same moment, Rachel grinned. 'You go first.'

He nodded. 'You know I think the world of you, Rachel. We've had a lot of great times together.'

'But?' she coaxed.

He appeared apologetic. 'But I don't think we're meant for each other.'

'You don't?' She wasn't trying to put him on the spot, but wanted to know his reasons so she could compare them to hers.

His expression became apologetic. 'What we had was good, but…' His voice faded.

'But it's better with Krissy,' she supplied.

His shoulders dropped and he seemed relieved by her grasp of his situation. 'Yeah. I'm sorry, Rachel.'

'Me, too,' she said softly. Although she knew their split was best for all concerned, it didn't mean that she didn't feel the sting of rejection or the loss of her dreams.

'It's for the best, though,' he said, his voice more confident.

'Yes, it is,' she said in all sincerity. 'How long have you known her?'

'Just a few weeks. I don't know if our relationship will go anywhere, but I'm hopeful.'

She rose, noticing he did the same. 'I'm happy for you, Charles,' she said, hugging him and realizing how their embrace seemed rather familial instead of passionate.

'Thank you.'

She stepped back. 'You'll keep in touch? Especially if you start to hear wedding bells?'

Pink inched its way across his face. 'Sure.' He drew his eyebrows together. 'What are your plans? Are you coming back to Wichita?'

'I have to,' she quipped. 'My things are still in my apartment.'

'Then you're not staying in Hooper?'

'I haven't decided. When I do, I'll let you know.'

The sound of Nick's and Krissy's voices reached them before the two reappeared around the corner. 'We probably should be going, Krissy,' Charles said. 'It's a long drive home.'

The two exchanged a glance, but Krissy didn't argue. 'I'm ready whenever you are.'

Nick and Charles shook hands. 'Thanks for the phone call,' Charles told him.

'My pleasure.'

The two strolled down the steps toward the car waiting near the curb. Rachel stood on the porch with Nick beside her, watching Charles open the door for Krissy. Calling out her goodbyes, she returned their waves, dropping her hand once Charles pulled into the line of traffic.

'That was quite a surprise you arranged,' she told Nick.

'Yeah, well, it wasn't *quite* what I had in mind,' he said, stuffing his hands in his trouser pockets. 'I had no idea that old Charlie would bring a guest. She isn't a relative, by any chance?'

'No,' she said wryly. 'She's not.'

He frowned. 'He's got some nerve,' he growled.

Rachel laid a hand on his arm. 'Calm down. It worked out rather well in the end.'

His tension eased. 'Did you, um, have a nice talk?'

'We talked. I'm not sure how nice it was.'

Nick's tone became tentative. 'I'll punch his lights out for you if that will make you feel better.'

Rachel pictured Nick, who outweighed Charles by at least thirty pounds and stood half a head taller, planting his fist in Charles's face. She giggled. 'You don't have to do that for me. Although right now, I can't decide if I feel sad or happy, relieved or disappointed.'

'Maybe it's all of the above.'

She closed her eyes and tried to label her emotions. 'Maybe you're right.'

'You know what the cure is?' he asked, slinging his arm around her shoulder and pulling her close.

Rachel stared up at him, enjoying the sensation of being tucked protectively under his arm. 'No, Doctor, I don't. What *is* the cure?'

'A kiss. Chocolate. A nap. Preferably in that order.'

'Sounds sinful. Where should I fill my prescription?'

His lopsided grin drove her last remaining thoughts of Charles completely out of her head. For the first time, she felt free to enjoy Nick and to dream of where the future might take them.

'Wherever you'd like,' he whispered, pulling her more fully into his embrace until she was pressed along his length and loving every moment of it.

'Don't you have patients to see?'

'When I thought the plumber was coming today, I left my schedule open.'

'But he came last week.'

'My receptionist didn't get the message about the change, so she didn't book any appointments. I'm free as a bird until after lunch.'

'Well, then,' she said, 'let's not waste any time.'

She raised herself on tiptoe in order to meet his mouth. Although she'd felt sparks dance between them before, she'd always held back because of Charles. Now, with their formal parting, she allowed herself to fan those embers into a blaze.

She forgot Krissy under the searing intensity of Nick's mouth against hers.

She forgot Charles as she felt the delicious roughness of Nick's tongue.

She forgot her surroundings as she explored his lean frame, running her hands across his back, enjoying the play of muscles under her hands, threading her fingers through the hair at his nape.

She forgot everything as his hands stroked her softness, pulling her against him so that she stood nestled within the V of his legs.

It seemed impossible for this much chemistry to flow between two people, much less that it flow between Nick and herself.

A shrill whistle brought her down to earth with a thump. Weak-kneed, she clung to Nick as she glanced in the direction of the noise. To her dismay, two boys, both about twelve and both on bicycles, had stopped on the sidewalk. Wide-eyed, they watched then sheepish grins crossed their faces.

Nick waved. 'Hi, boys. Fine day for a ride, isn't it?'

'Sure is,' the taller said as he nudged the smaller. 'We'd better go now.'

'Bye,' Nick called out.

But as they started pedaling, their bike chains squealing, Rachel heard their comments quite clearly.

'Wow, my mom and dad don't ever kiss that like.'

'Bet they do. You're here, aren't you?'

'Yeah, but kissing a girl? Yuck.'

As the pair's voices faded, Rachel leaned her head against Nick's chest and felt his rumble of laughter. 'Can you imagine what they're going to tell their parents?'

'Yeah. And it would be the honest-to-gosh truth.'

'How did you get to be such a good kisser?' she asked, inhaling his unique scent and branding it in her memory.

'Some people just bring out the best in others,' he teased. 'Now comes the second part of my prescription.'

'The nap?' she asked, hoping that she wouldn't take it alone.

'Not yet,' he said. 'I'm saving the best for last.'

A shiver of anticipation slid down her spine. 'When?'

'Later,' he promised. 'That phase can't be rushed.'

'I do like your orders, Doctor.'

'You should,' he said. 'I wrote them with you in mind.'

'Can I have refills?'

'As many as you want.'

At noon, Rachel sat at the kitchen table with a bowl of chocolate ice cream in front of her. Nick would soon be leaving for his office, but she'd slipped into a pair of comfortable shorts and a top that revealed the colorful bruises on her shoulder.

'Too bad you can't take the afternoon off, too,' she said, using her spoon to twirl circles along the top scoop of her ice cream.

'Don't tempt me. It's just as well, though.' Nick sat in the chair across the table from her.

'Why do you say that?'

'Because you wouldn't get your rest.' He pointed to her bowl. 'Eat.'

'Bossy as ever,' she grumbled, although she obediently took a bite.

'Yup. Now, this afternoon, I want you to—'

She held up her hands. 'Now, wait a minute. I know what I need to do.'

He raised one eyebrow. 'Oh?'

'Yes. I'm going to choose our wallpaper.'

'OK, but see if you can find room for some of my things.'

She stared at him. 'What for?'

'I'm moving in. Any objections?'

'Well, no,' she began. Truthfully, she was both excited and anxious at the prospect. 'Aren't we rushing a bit?'

Nick smiled as if he understood the doubts running through her head. 'Although I'd like to sleep with you, that isn't the main reason I'm staying.'

'It isn't?'

He shot her a I-can't-believe-you-haven't-figured-it-out look. 'The police haven't caught the guy who broke in. If he comes back, I don't want you here alone.'

'I have to be by myself some time,' she said practically, although she was touched by his concern. 'Besides, he won't be back. The article is slated for tonight's newspaper.'

'It doesn't hurt to be prepared,' he insisted.

'What will my grandparents say? Hooper has small town values. People will be appalled, shocked, horrified if—'

'Get serious, Rach. They watch television. And even if they didn't, it's none of their business.' As she opened her mouth to protest, he added, 'As great as our kisses are, you can rest easy. For now, I'll sleep on the couch. Mark my words, though. I *am* spending this night and every other night here until they find the fellow.'

She was thrilled…and terrified…and so focused on his 'for now' reference that she jumped at the sound of the doorbell. 'I'll get it,' she said.

A brunette about Rachel's age stood on the porch, although Rachel didn't recognize her. 'Hi,' she said, wondering if she might be Jack's daughter who was reported to be coming back once the doctor released him from the hospital's long-term care unit.

The woman smiled as she returned Rachel's greeting. 'If you have a few minutes free, I'd like to visit with you. It's important.'

Rachel welcomed her in and Nick met them in the living room. 'Theresa,' he said jovially. 'What brings you here?'

'I came to ask if Rachel might be interested in a job at Hooper General.'

Rachel was stunned, too stunned, in fact, to do more than say, 'What?'

'I'm the director of nursing,' Theresa explained. 'It's come to my attention from various sources that you're a nurse.'

'Yes, I am, but—'

'I also understand that you've worked in the ER.'

'Yes, but—' Rachel stared helplessly at Nick, but he simply shrugged.

Theresa glanced at Nick although she addressed Rachel. 'I don't know if you're aware, but one of our ER nurses is pregnant and has gone into premature labor. She's on bed rest until her due date, which is in three weeks.'

'I don't see what that has to do with me.'

'I need a temporary replacement,' Theresa said. 'I'm already stretched to breaking point, as you already know from your stay this past weekend. I need someone with experience to fill Merrilee's shoes until she comes back from maternity leave. You would work the day shift, seven to three.'

Rachel opened her mouth to object, but Theresa continued before she could. 'I know you're busy with other things…' she glanced around the room '…but we really need you. Would you think about my offer and let me know as soon as possible…?'

Nick broke in. 'She will.'

Theresa's face registered her relief. 'Thank you.'

The moment the door closed with a quiet snick behind her, Rachel turned on Nick. 'What do you mean by ''She will''? You can't make those decisions for me.'

'I didn't make your decision,' he said patiently. 'You have the option to refuse. I only said you'd think about her request.'

Rachel placed her hands on her hips. 'I don't have to think. I know what I want to do.'

'Which is?'

'I can't work there. Especially not in ER.'

'Why not?'

She met his gaze. 'You know why.'

His smile was tender. 'You're a strong person, Rachel. You can lick this.'

'I've tried. I wasn't strong enough.'

'Give yourself a chance.'

'I don't want to get involved. What if...?' Her thought went unspoken.

'What if someone dies because you *aren't* there to use your knowledge and expertise?'

She squared her shoulders and crossed her arms. 'I'm not going back.'

'I know you're afraid,' he said. 'But you've always had plenty of courage.'

'Not any more.'

'Yes, you do,' he insisted. 'Courage comes about when we act under terrifying circumstances. To paraphrase Mark Twain, courage isn't an absence of fear—it's about resisting that fear and mastering it.' He paused. 'You can do it.'

She drew a deep breath. 'As difficult as it is for you to imagine, this time you're wrong.'

CHAPTER NINE

'WHY does he *do* that?'

Rachel sat at her grandmother's table and flicked the pull tab of her soda can with her fingernail. She should have been spending the last several hours mulling over Theresa's offer, but she couldn't get past the way Nick had so high-handedly spoken for her. She still bristled with frustration whenever she thought about it.

Sitting at home, alone with her thoughts, hadn't helped matters. With Nick at his office, she'd sought her only other place of refuge—her grandmother's.

'Why does who do what, dear?' Hester placed a plate of gingerbread cookies in front of Rachel, which she ignored.

'Nick. He always pokes his nose in my affairs,' she said. 'I was prepared to refuse Theresa's offer. He had no right to tell her that I would think about it.'

'What's wrong with that? He was only trying to save you from a decision you might regret later.'

'I don't need him to save me,' she countered. 'Besides, my "no" wouldn't have been impulsive. You forget that I debated my choices before I even came to Hooper. Why can't Nick accept that?'

'Because he's as strong-willed as you are. Be honest, dear. How would you *really* like to respond to your job offer?'

Much as she hated to admit it, Nick's comments had chipped away enough fragments of her stubborn attitude so that now she felt adrift. 'I don't have the slightest idea.'

'Of course you do, dear. I'd hazard a guess that the only reason you're balking is because you know Nick wants you to accept.' She gentled her voice. 'It's time you understood something. Nick has always had your best interests at heart, which is why he pushed you not to settle for second best. Remember your speech class and your stint as a hospital volunteer?'

Rachel recalled how he'd talked her into enrolling in the high-school course because she'd been deathly afraid of speaking in front of a group. She'd also volunteered at the hospital because Nick had convinced her to check out potential medical careers.

'Those experiences got you where you are today.'

Grudgingly, Rachel agreed. At the time, she'd sworn that he'd bullied her into those situations because he'd done what had come naturally, but in retrospect she might have misread his motives.

She sighed. 'Everything is so confusing.'

Hester nodded. 'Your focus is all wrong. Once you change your perspective, you'll see your way clearly.'

'But I've lost my edge.'

Hester raised one eyebrow. 'Have you really?'

'You're starting to sound like Mrs Parker. She was in the hospital room near mine and we talked one evening to pass the time.'

'If I know Eleanor, she didn't mince her words. What did she tell you?'

Rachel tried to recall what the old woman had said as best she could. 'She mentioned how we usually find whatever we lose and how sometimes it's hiding in plain sight.'

'My point exactly,' Hester said triumphantly. 'It's all a matter of how you view a situation.'

'Nick said that, too.' His challenge of how someone might die because she *wasn't* there to help still rang in her ears.

'He's right.'

'Perhaps,' she countered. 'But why am I having so much trouble making up my mind?'

'Well, dear, I dare say you've convinced yourself that

you're a failure, but you're not. You've simply suffered a setback.'

'No, Grams. It's not a setback. I've lost faith in myself.'

'That may be,' Hester said gently. 'The question is, do you honestly believe you'll restore it by painting and wall-papering?' Before Rachel could answer, she leaned forward. 'Nick's always been an achiever and met his trials head on. You know that as well as I.'

'Yes, but this isn't his trial. It's mine.'

Hester laughed. 'Yes, it is. However, you need to realize one thing. You may have lost faith in yourself, but Nick hasn't. Be glad that he doesn't think you're beyond salvaging.'

Hester sat back and continued, 'Since you came to talk, and I presume to hear a few words of wisdom, I'm going to make a suggestion of my own. If you lose something, where do you look for it?'

Rachel gritted her teeth in exasperation. 'I didn't misplace my car keys.'

'Humor me. Now, if you've lost something,' Hester repeated, 'where will you look?'

Her grandmother wouldn't rest until Rachel played the game, so she did. 'I'd backtrack to the last place where I had it.'

Hester straightened, a triumphant gleam on her face. 'Does that tell you anything?'

The lesson and its symbolism finally made sense. Was it possible that she'd find her answers in ER? Even as she considered the possibility, she dismissed it. 'I stayed in ER for almost a month after Grace and Molly died. If your theory is correct, I shouldn't have needed to quit in the first place.'

'Ah, but you're forgetting something,' Hester answered. 'We don't always find what we're looking for on the first try. It's all in the timing.'

Rachel still wasn't convinced. Her grandmother, however, obviously wasn't willing to concede defeat.

'I know you're worried and frightened, but you've taken your break and now you're due back in the game. If you wait too long, you never will return, and you'll always wonder, "what if…?"'

Although she recognized the truth in her grandmother's statement, she asked, 'Will you be disappointed if I refuse the hospital's offer?'

'I know how much your nursing degree meant to you,' she said kindly. 'You're a born helper, Rachel. Nick noticed that quality in you long ago, which was why he convinced you to volunteer at the hospital. He suspected you'd be hooked, and he was right.'

'Really? *That* was why he kept hounding me to sign up?'

Hester smiled. 'Those were his exact words. What you called nagging was actually his way of encouraging you. You have to admit, you were the quiet, methodical, remain-in-the-background type. Being a high achiever himself, Nick wanted you to reach your full potential, and if he had to prod you, he was more than willing to do so.'

'I never realized….' Rachel began. She'd attributed his methods to being bossy and controlling. Was her grandmother right? Had he acted in that way for her own good and not because he was a person who thrived on dominating others?

'In any event,' Hester continued, 'if you want to switch careers, we certainly won't stand in your way. Just make sure you do it for the right reasons. Everyone, from your sisters to your grandfather and I, only wants you to be happy.'

Emotion clogged Rachel's throat as she knew that, no matter what direction she took, she still had her family's support. She rose and kissed her grandmother on her cheek. 'Thanks for listening, Grams. Tell Grandpa hi when he gets home.'

Later, too keyed to rest, she spent the remainder of the afternoon thumbing through the wallcovering books. Nick would want to know her decision the moment he walked through the door, but she wasn't ready to commit herself. Nick may have always pushed her so that she wouldn't settle for second best, but she wondered how far he'd go this time.

As she stared at the colorful samples, an idea came to her. If properly planned, she could finally teach Nick that he couldn't manipulate her without facing the consequences.

Nick strode into the house at six o'clock with a fair amount of wariness filling him. Rachel hadn't been too happy over what she perceived as his interference and now that she'd spent all afternoon by herself, he wondered if he'd need some form of protection—maybe a suit of armor—when she saw him again.

He found her in the kitchen, assembling sandwiches. 'Hi,' he said, wishing he felt free enough to grab her around her waist and kiss her senseless. Until he discovered her mood and she wasn't holding a knife in her hand, he didn't dare. 'How has your afternoon been?'

His worries evaporated under her wide and seemingly genuine smile. He should have known better than to doubt her. Rachel wasn't the type of person who held a grudge—one more thing he loved about her.

'Busy,' she said. 'I visited my grandmother, looked at wallpaper samples and made a quick trip to the grocery store.'

'You were supposed to be resting. If I recall, the third part of my prescription was a nap.' If his office could have spared him, he would have ensured that she followed his orders. Then again, if he'd been able to take their earlier kiss to its natural conclusion, they wouldn't have spent the time sleeping.

'Visiting with people is restful,' she countered. 'So is looking at the sample books. Want to see the designs I've chosen?'

'Sure. Why not?' Nick's fears of having to duck utensils

completely disappeared. Mondays being what they usually were in his office, he was ready for a relaxing evening with Rachel.

'I'll show you after we've eaten,' she told him. 'If you freshen up, we'll dig in.'

'What's the rush?'

'We need to measure all the rooms so we know how many rolls of paper to order and gallons of paint to buy.'

'You think we'll agree on what we want in one evening?'

'I know we will.' Rachel handed him a loaded plate. 'Dinner is now served.'

Her confidence surprised him, but he refused to spoil the genial mood which lasted throughout their quick meal.

Thirty minutes later, he sat on the sofa and eyed the stack of bound sample books lying on the coffee-table. From the number of paper slips stuck in the spines of the books, he would be sitting there for quite some time.

'All right,' he said, 'show me what you've come up with.'

'OK, but I want you to hold your comments until the end.'

'I will.'

Sitting beside him, she started with the smallest upstairs bedroom, outlining her ideas with the same thoroughness a marketing expert would have used in a professional presentation. As she moved onto the next room, he took great pains to hide his opinions about her predominant use of pink and purple. By the time she had spelled out her plans for literally every inch of the house, he could hardly contain himself.

'What do you think?' she asked.

'I can tell you put a lot of thought into this—' he began.

'There's a "but" coming. I can hear it.'

He winced at her droll tone. 'It's just that the decor seems so…pink and so…*busy*.' He pointed to a page containing such a hodgepodge of flowers and leaves that it was like looking at a 3-D poster. 'I was hoping for something easier on the eyes.'

'Which is why I purposely chose the small flower patterns instead of the one with a more magnified design.'

Nick hated to veto her suggestions since she'd clearly worked hard on co-ordinating the prints. At the same time, he found it hard to believe that their tastes ran so far apart. 'Yes, but there's so much...*plant* life. Roses and—'

'Notice how the hall will have a variety of flowers and each room will showcase a specific type. I thought it sounded neat to have a Rose Room and a Lilac Room and a—'

'You've done a wonderful job,' he said, trying to give her credit although he thought she'd gone overboard with the floral motif. Flowers belonged in a garden or on a table, not on every wall. 'The ivy border is nice, but I don't think it should be in every room.'

'I'm also going to carry the design through the lower level,' she said.

He swallowed hard. 'Are you sure that's a good idea? People could walk through the entire house and feel like they were being strangled.'

'Don't be ridiculous,' she said calmly. 'Running the ivy border gives a sense of continuity. As for feeling strangled, it wouldn't be any worse than waking up at night in the middle of a jungle. Although,' she said thoughtfully, 'we could use the animal preserve print in the hall and then feature certain animals in each room. I think I saw something with deer and trout in one of these books.'

He grabbed her hand and stopped her search. 'Scratch the jungle print. No trout and deer rooms either.'

Rachel rolled her eyes. 'No flowers and no animals. You're going to have to work with me here. What *do* you want?'

'What's wrong with stripes?'

'Nothing, if you want the house to look like a candy cane. Do you know what your problem is?'

'No, but you're going to tell me, aren't you?'

'You can't accept any ideas other than your own.'

'I can, too.'

She rolled her eyes. 'When was the last time?'

He opened his mouth to give an example, but his mind went blank. 'I can't think of the situation right now.'

She shot a superior look at him. 'I rest my case.'

'If I remember correctly, you didn't like to compromise either.'

'Only because *I* was the one who had to give in every time. I'm willing to concede on some things, but you have to, too.'

He accepted her challenge. 'Let the negotiations begin.'

'First, tell me what you like.'

'Well,' he began, struggling to find something that appealed to him, 'the seashells in the bathroom are appropriate.' He didn't mention that he would have preferred the same pattern in hunter green rather than peach, but he could live with either color. 'Drop those purple things in the east bedroom and use the stripes that look like crayon marks.'

'The ivy pattern doesn't match the stripes.'

'So don't use ivy in that room.'

'Then it ruins my decorating theme.'

'Who said we had to have a theme in the first place? If the colors blend together, why bother?'

'We're striving for a broad appeal,' she reminded him.

'I'm willing to have a few flowers,' he said, feeling as if he'd made a major concession. 'The roses can stay, but those lilac things and the ivy have to go.'

She crossed her legs and started to swing her ankle. 'You're forgetting something.'

'What?'

'Compromise means equal give and take. You've conceded on the roses, so I'll forget the lilacs. What are you willing to trade for the ivy?'

He thought a moment. 'I don't know.'

'We do have a problem, then, don't we?' She sounded far too cheerful for his comfort.

'I'd say so.'

Rachel tapped one finger on her temple. 'There is another possibility.'

'Which is?'

'Am I correct in assuming that you want me to tell Theresa I'll accept her temporary job offer?'

It took him a moment to follow the abrupt subject change. 'We're talking about the house.'

'Just answer the question.'

'Of course I want you to accept her job offer,' he said impatiently. 'Not only does the hospital need you, you're wasting everything you've ever worked for.'

'All right.' Her satisfied tone warned him of a trap about to close in on him. 'I'll work for Theresa until Merrilee comes back from maternity leave *if* you'll let me decorate the house, no questions asked.'

'Those are two unrelated situations.'

'I've linked them together.'

Suddenly he saw right through her plan and hid his smile. Rachel had proposed such preposterous ideas because she expected him to refuse, thereby taking her off the proverbial hook with Theresa. 'Let me get this straight. If I don't let you choose the wallpaper, you won't work at the hospital.'

'You got it. Furthermore, if I stay at home, you can't hound me about it either.'

'Sounds more like blackmail than a compromise.'

She smiled. 'Call it what you will. So what's it going to be?'

Helping Rachel find her courage meant more to him than having ivy and lilacs on the walls of a house he wouldn't live in anyway. The only reason he felt strongly about the interior design was because the house had become more than a building to renovate. It had become theirs—his and Rachel's.

'OK,' he said simply. 'You have a deal. The nursing job for the wallpaper.'

He knew she hadn't expected his answer when he saw her eyes widen and her mouth drop. 'You're serious?'

'It sounds like a fair trade.'

'But—'

Nick smiled broadly. 'You didn't think I would agree, did you?'

'No,' she said slowly. 'No, I didn't.' Then, 'Why did you?'

'You're more important than wallpaper and color schemes and ivy. So I officially give you free rein, but I expect you to call Theresa first thing in the morning.'

Rachel still appeared stunned. 'I will.'

Because he didn't see Rachel as being a die-hard pastel-type person, he asked, 'Now, are you going to show me what you *really* have in mind?'

Her eyes narrowed. 'You knew I'd staged this?'

'I suspected as much after you tied the house and the hospital together. Even then, I wasn't positive until I saw your reaction when I accepted your terms.' As she tried to speak and couldn't, he knew he'd totally flustered her. 'Do I get to see the actual plans?'

'You'll see them soon enough,' she said tartly. 'Why?'

'No reason. I was thinking about buying the house, though.'

'You?'

'I can't live in the garage apartment for ever.'

'Yes, but you want to buy *this* house? These aren't bachelor's quarters. This is a place for a family.'

'I don't intend to remain single for ever.'

'Oh.'

With lightning-bolt speed, it occurred to him that whoever had coined the saying 'Nothing ventured, nothing gained' had certainly known what he or she had been talking about. Granted, he risked their friendship once he made his feelings known, but he couldn't expect Rachel to take risks if he wasn't willing to do the same.

He drew a deep breath. 'Want to know who I'm hoping will want to move in with me?'

A pained expression spread across her face before she raised a sardonic eyebrow. 'You've already picked her out of your legions?'

In that instant, he wondered if her constant references to the women he'd dated was simply a defense against her own jealousy. Suspecting it was, he nodded. 'Yes, I have.' He gazed at her tenderly. 'It's you.'

'Me?' she squealed.

He reached over to grab her hands. 'You,' he said firmly.

Rachel stared at him in numbed silence. 'What about the girl you referred to as being your failure?'

'She was you,' he answered.

She blinked in obvious shock. 'Me?' she asked, her voice hoarse.

He nodded, uncertain how she felt. He dug himself into his hole of commitment a little deeper. 'I love you, Rachel.'

'How can you say that?' she asked. 'We're always at odds.'

'Did you ever wonder why?'

'Because you had to be the final authority? The man in charge?'

Nick laughed. 'They say that love and hate are only a whit apart. My theory is that we couldn't express our feelings, so we squabbled in order to defuse those tensions. If we truly hated each other, we wouldn't have remained friends all those years.'

'But I'm not like those other girls…other women…'

'Thank goodness you're not,' he said fervently.

Tears suddenly shone in Rachel's eyes and the smile on her face couldn't have been any more dazzling. His fears of hearing her rejection eased. 'Oh, Nick. I don't know what to say.'

'An "I love you, too" would be nice. Or a kiss. I'd be happy with either response.'

Just when he was ready to congratulate himself for taking the plunge, Rachel covered her face and burst into tears.

Panic set in. 'What's wrong?'

'Everything,' she mumbled. 'Nothing. Your lousy timing.'

'My…'

'I have so much going on in my life right now,' she told him in between her sniffles. 'I can't take it all in…'

Her voice faded as he drew her close to tuck her head under his chin, his own dread subsiding. 'I realize you have a lot on your mind and your bump on the head isn't helping matters—'

'You can say that again,' she muttered. 'Any minute I'll wake up and discover this has been a dream.'

'You're not dreaming,' he said firmly, pulling her with him as he sank against the cushions.

The tension in her body eased and she snuggled closer. 'This certainly doesn't feel like a dream.'

A specific portion of his anatomy could attest to that. So could his suddenly sweaty palms and dry throat. He would have liked nothing better than to carry Rachel to her bedroom, follow her onto the mattress and explore every beautiful inch of her. Then he wanted to take her on a trip to scale the heights before they drifted back to earth where they could recuperate before repeating the process.

Nick forced himself not to dwell on those thoughts. Rachel hadn't completely recovered from her concussion and, having just come home from the hospital, he would be totally insensitive to her needs if he placed his own first.

But, oh, how he wanted to.

Steady, he thought. He could be patient. Barely. He contented himself with holding her until she started to move away. He reluctantly let her go.

'I can't begin to tell you how happy you've made me,' she said, but her next expression was apologetic, as was her tone. 'But I've realized I'm not ready to make any promises or long-term plans yet, Nick. I'd like to, and if our paths had crossed a year ago, I wouldn't hesitate for a single moment. Unfortunately, I don't know where I'll be in a few months or what I'll be doing. Chances are good that I won't even be here.'

The thought of Rachel leaving sent a chill down his spine and he hid his worry behind humor. 'You don't think I can convince you to stay?'

'I expect you'll try,' she said wryly. 'However, I can't begin to contemplate a relationship when my life is a mess.'

'Not a mess,' he corrected. 'A transition.'

She shrugged as if unconvinced by his assessment. 'To be honest, I feel guilty whenever I think of a relationship.'

'Charles wasn't the man for you, Rachel.' He met her gaze. 'We both know that.'

She hesitated. 'Actually, I wasn't referring to Charles.'

If it wasn't Charles... 'Then who?'

'It's Grace.'

He struggled to comprehend how a dead woman—God rest her soul—could prevent Rachel from entering into a relationship with him. 'I don't follow you.'

'Grace was starting a whole new life with a man who loved her and her daughter. I feel responsible for that not happening. It doesn't seem fair for me to be happy when she...' Her voice broke and she bit her lip.

'Punishing yourself won't bring her back,' he said gently. 'You've already given up the career you loved and now you want to avoid having a satisfying future with someone who loves you. I didn't know your friend, but I doubt if she would want your life to end because hers did.'

'It must be nice to have all the answers,' she said cynically.

'I don't,' he said. 'I just call things like I see 'em.'

Rachel sighed. 'I have so many unresolved issues. I don't know where or how to begin to sort through them.'

'Time has a way of handling our problems for us.'

'Then you won't mind if we put our relationship on hold?'

'Yes, I do mind,' he stated firmly. 'Time marches on and seasons change. We have to move forward. On the other hand, we'll take things slow…'

'Good idea,' she said.

'I don't quite agree,' he said in a dry tone, aware of how close he came to bursting with unfulfilled need whenever they were together. 'I'd like nothing more than to haul you into the nearest bedroom before I carry you in front of a justice of the peace, but I'll force myself to wait.'

Her cheeks turned pink under Nick's intense and unflinching gaze. He wanted her to see that he meant every word.

'It's been a long day and I think you should turn in,' he said, trying to push away his mental picture of her sleeping.

'We haven't measured the walls.'

'They can wait.'

'No,' she insisted. 'It won't take that long. If I go to bed now, I'll toss and turn all night.'

He was ready to refuse, then remembered what she'd said about compromise. 'You win. We'll start measuring,' he said. 'But the minute I think you're overdoing things, we stop. Regardless of how much or how little we've accomplished.'

'I can accept those terms.' Her smile was reflected in her eyes. 'See how painless it is to give and take? Maybe we'll get through the rest of the night without arguing.'

He smiled. 'I don't know. I enjoy having differences of opinion.'

'You do?'

'Sure. You get this little dimple right here…' he pointed to her left cheek '…and your eyes start to shoot fire, and you turn this gorgeous shade of pink.'

'I thought you didn't like pink.'

'On you, Rachel, it's my favorite color.'

*   *   *

Rachel agreed to start at the hospital two days later. Certain Nick wouldn't approve, she greeted him as he came home on Tuesday evening with a searing kiss. In spite of her attempt to make him mellow before she announced her plans, he'd still objected most strenuously.

'You can't go tomorrow,' he said with a trace of finality. 'As your doctor, I won't release you.'

'But you're not my physician,' she pointed out with some glee. 'Dylan is and I've already discussed it with him. For your information, he wanted me to come in this afternoon.'

'I always thought he was a quack,' Nick muttered.

Rachel laughed. 'You don't and you know it. Besides, I thought you'd be thrilled because I'm not procrastinating.'

'I am, but I'd be even more thrilled if your energy level was where it should be. I saw you at noon today and you were looking peaked.'

'I'm only working half-days for the rest of the week.'

'That's better,' he grumbled. 'So, are we redoing the steps this evening?'

'Absolutely. Mr Bates delivered the lumber this afternoon, so we're all set.' She eyed his short-sleeved shirt and chinos. 'As soon as you're more presentable, that is.'

Immediately he pulled his shirt from the waistband of his pants, stripped off his tie and began unbuttoning his shirt. The sight of his bare chest was enough to make a grown woman drool. 'Your work clothes are on top of the dryer,' she added.

He wiggled his eyebrows. 'Want to help me get undressed?'

'I think you can manage,' she said.

At his crestfallen but obviously feigned look, she grinned. 'I'll meet you on the front porch.'

'Spoilsport.'

Yet, as she went outside, she knew if she'd stayed in the kitchen a moment longer, she would have followed him into the bedroom and rescheduled this particular project for another time. Ever since he'd declared his love for her, the awareness she experienced in his presence now flooded over her instantly and with all the force of an F-5 tornado. A simple touch, a single glance, the sound of his gentle breathing as he slept on the couch—all stirred her to the point where her body felt lighter than air.

Little did Nick know that the reason she'd been so tired was because she hadn't been able to sleep at night. Not because she was afraid the intruder or his cronies might return, but because it took every ounce of her will-power to keep from inviting him to her room. The sight of him as he came out of the shower wearing a pair of low-riding boxer shorts would have tested a saint. It was pure torture to see his broad expanse of skin and the dusting of hair that dipped below his navel.

Although he'd agreed to take things slowly, his kisses were the opposite. They were filled with hunger and passion and pure need. If Rachel had known that guilt wouldn't surface during those initial 'morning-after' moments, she would have been more than eager to let herself love him in the fullest sense possible.

Unfortunately, her self-blame always managed to rear its ugly head just when temptation struck. Perhaps Nick was right. Perhaps she was subconsciously punishing herself for Grace's life being cut short, but she didn't know how to move past those feelings, consign them to yesterday and look to the future.

One thing was certain. She loved Nick and finally understood why Marta and Amy epitomized her grandmother's description of being 'as happy as ducks in water.'

She fell asleep dreaming of the day when she might be just as content as her sisters. For the first time since Nick had started to spend the night in the house, she slept well.

The circles under her eyes must have disappeared because the next day Dylan remarked on the change. 'You look chipper this morning.'

'I am.' Although she sensed he was fishing for personal

details, she stuck to more mundane topics. 'We replaced the porch steps last night. The air conditioning people are installing the unit today, and as soon as the wallpaper comes in we'll be working on my favorite part—the decorating.'

'Sounds as if you're almost finished,' he said.

'Only with the upstairs. The first level doesn't have any structural problems, so we only have to update the decor. It will take several months before we're completely done.' Maybe by then she would know if she had her confidence back. If not, she'd walk away once and for all, although she hoped she wouldn't be forced to walk away from Nick as well. For the time being, she didn't want to dwell on that unpleasant thought.

She spent the rest of the morning becoming orientated to the department. Bonnie, a newly minted graduate nurse who hadn't yet received the results of her certification exams, showed her the supply cupboard and gave her a quick run-down on their computer system. Luckily, it wasn't too different from the one Rachel was accustomed to and by lunchtime she felt comfortable enough to navigate it by herself.

In spite of how well she thought her first day went, she was more than ready to go home.

By the end of the week, however, she was in the swing of things and when an ambulance call came right before noon on Friday, she opted to stay in spite of her clammy hands and her rapid heartbeat. She had to deal with this aspect of her work, and because she was new in town the odds were good that the victim wouldn't be someone she knew.

'You'll need me,' she told Dylan and Theresa, trying to convince herself, too. 'We've already seen a lot of cases, most of them minor, but you need an extra pair of hands.' Grateful for her assistance, they didn't argue.

The patient who'd come via the emergency vehicle was a thirty-two-year-old electrical lineman whose safety belt had snapped while he'd been working at the top of a pole. His twenty-foot fall had netted him a sliced hand, as he'd tried to grab the foot pegs, a broken wrist, a dislocated hip, a fractured femur and multiple scratches from landing in a euonymus bush. Most concerning however, was his possible spinal injury. Without MRI capabilities, Dylan and the radiologist were hard pressed to tell the extent of the damage with any real certainty.

Groggy from the pain medication, Rick Jones slurred his words to ask, 'Is my wife here yet?'

'I understand she's on her way,' Rachel said.

'How bad is it?'

Dylan listed his injuries.

'My legs hurt and I can't feel my toes, Doc,' Rick said.

'It could be because of the broken bones,' Dylan answered, exchanging a glance with Rachel across his bed. 'However, I have to warn you. Your spinal cord may be damaged.'

'Damaged? How bad?'

'It may only be bruised,' Dylan said. 'Unfortunately, without an MRI, we can't tell for sure. If the spinal column is bruised, there's a good chance you'll regain feeling and once the bones heal you'll be as good as new.'

'If it's not?'

'Then you'll need special care and rehabilitation,' Dylan said. 'But don't buy a wheelchair yet. Paralysis is only one of the possibilities. The staff at Joplin will be able to assess the damage more accurately than we can here.'

Dylan motioned to Rachel and she followed him outside. 'I'll make the arrangements for his transfer. Once his wife arrives, find me.'

'I will,' she promised.

She returned to Rick Jones's side and busied herself with recording his vital signs and gathering his radiology records to send along with him.

'Don't s'pose I'll be climbing poles any more,' he said. 'Can't do that if I'm crippled.'

'Now, you don't know that for certain,' she said. 'Spinal cord injuries can fool you. Don't give up hope already.'

'I'm trying not to,' he said, 'but the thought of being a burden to my wife and kids…'

'Worry about it when you have to and not a moment before,' she advised.

A few minutes later, Mrs Jones arrived. Rachel gave her a few private moments with her husband while she found Dylan. Later, after he'd explained the extent of her husband's injuries and she dealt with the paperwork, Mrs Jones approached Rachel at the nurses' station.

'Can I talk to you for a minute?'

'Of course,' Rachel said, leading her to the meditation room at the north end of the ER. 'What can I help you with?'

'Dr Gower says Rick may have spinal cord injuries,' she began.

'It's possible,' Rachel said, 'but not definite.'

'You're not giving me false hope, are you?'

'No, I'm not,' Rachel said gently. 'If we knew beyond all doubt that your husband's cord was severed, Dr Gower would tell you. But we're not one hundred per cent positive. However, it wouldn't be fair to you if we didn't prepare you for the possibility.'

'I guess there's always hope.'

'Yes, there is.' A sense of *déjà vu* came over Rachel. With luck, Mrs Jones wouldn't lose her confidence like Rachel had.

Tears flooded the woman's eyes. 'I feel so guilty about this.'

'Why?'

Mrs Jones looked away. 'We argued before Rick left the house this morning. He's normally meticulous about his equipment. Today, he wasn't.'

'Do you know that for sure? Is that what your husband said?'

'N-no.'

'But you think his accident is your fault.'

'Don't you see?' Mrs Jones was frantic. 'If he hadn't been so upset over the things I said, he wouldn't have been preoccupied. He would have stayed focused.'

'Maybe he forgot about your argument and his safety harness simply failed. Accidents do happen.'

'I don't think it's that simple. If he's paralyzed, it will be my fault and I'll never forgive myself.'

Rachel took her hand. 'Look,' she said kindly, 'is your husband experienced in what he does?'

'He's been a lineman for nearly twelve years,' she said proudly.

'Then he knew what he was doing. Don't take responsibility for something you had no control over.'

'I suppose you're right. It's hard not to believe that I didn't contribute to…' Her voice choked. 'To his accident.'

'I know,' Rachel said, empathizing far more than Mrs Jones could imagine. 'But you can't dwell on what happened. He's going to need you more than ever, and if you're wallowing in guilt you won't help his recovery.'

Mrs Jones squared her shoulders and slowly nodded. 'Thanks for listening. I'll try to remember what you said.'

Rachel smiled. 'Good luck.' Then, as the woman returned to her husband's side, Rachel wondered why she couldn't follow her own advice. Life would be easier if she did.

CHAPTER TEN

THE Jones couple preyed on Rachel's mind while she went to the cafeteria for a snack and something to drink other than what they passed off as coffee. Dylan had called the hospital in Joplin for a status report and had learned a few minutes earlier that Rick Jones's spinal column was intact and he would walk again once his leg injuries healed. The news came as a relief since she and Mrs Jones had both been initiated into the Guilt Association. At least the other woman's membership had only been temporary.

She returned in time to hear another ambulance pull into the driveway. Leaving her cup of raspberry-flavored tea on the counter, she rushed onto the dock with Bonnie and Dylan.

As the EMTs opened their cargo bay doors and Rachel saw the small form on the stretcher, her heart sank down to her toes. It was a child, a toddler to be more precise, and an EMT was monitoring her oxygen flow. In spite of the mask, the child was white and her hands and feet were cyanotic.

Rachel swallowed the bile in her throat and focused on what the female driver was telling her as they pulled the stretcher out of the ambulance.

'Three-year-old girl fell into a swimming pool. The father had pulled her out and started CPR by the time we'd arrived. We have a pulse, but her respirations aren't good.'

'How long was she underwater?' Dylan asked.

'The parents think it was about two minutes. Give or take.'

Rachel knew that most submersions were fatal after two

to three minutes. Maybe this little girl would have a lucky break.

In no time at all they had moved her into a trauma room, yanked the curtains around the bed and closed the glass doors while the parents, who appeared to be Rachel's age, paced outside.

'Her BP is falling,' Bonnie called out.

'Pulse is weak and thready,' Rachel added.

'I want plasma on the double,' Dylan ordered.

'I've lost her heartbeat,' Rachel said. Dylan immediately began CPR again while one of the EMTs rushed to pull the code-blue cart closer.

In spite of all of Dylan's measures to restart the little girl's heart, it refused to co-operate. Finally, he straight-ened, drew a deep breath and shook his head.

'That's it.' He glanced at the wall clock. 'Time of death, two thirty-one.' With his normally jovial face set in grim lines, he meticulously stripped off his gloves while Rachel and the three other people stood like statues beside the child's body. After the last snap of the latex, he drew a deep breath and walked out of the room to break the news to the distraught parents.

The mother's wail came a few seconds later. Rachel stared at the youngster who'd been someone's pride and joy and felt the warmth of tears welling in her eyes. Her own breath came in spurts as she removed the pediatric mask, noticing the child's perfect features, the cute little button nose and the baby-fine blonde hair.

'What was her name?' she choked out.

'It was Cassie.' The woman EMT spoke in a clipped tone as she and her partner gathered their equipment with jerky movements. A minute later, they left Rachel to her own bitter tasks.

While Bonnie began stowing their own equipment, Rachel disconnected the IV line from the tiny hand that would no longer clutch her favorite toy or her mother's fingers. She took a sheet and covered the body, making the little girl appear like a life-sized doll who'd been placed in bed for a nap.

A nap from which she would never awaken.

Don't think about that, she told herself sternly, struggling for composure. As soon as she had nearly everything in order, she stepped around the curtain and strode toward the meditation room where family members could be counseled during a crisis. She caught Dylan's attention and simply nodded.

He understood her silent message because a few minutes later he escorted the little girl's parents to the trauma room where they could spend time alone with their daughter.

'I've called the chaplain,' Rachel said as he sank into a chair beside her.

'Good.'

She felt his gaze land on her.

'How are you doing?' he asked softly.

If he hadn't asked her that question, she would have been fine. Instead, his caring tone suddenly made her stomach churn. The emotion she'd been holding at bay battled against her control until it won. She darted into the rest-room around the corner, draped herself over the commode and sobbed until her chest hurt. After a seemingly long interval, her tears slowed to short hiccups. She didn't want to go back, but she couldn't hide in the restroom for the remainder of her shift. Through sheer force of will, she pulled herself together, washed her face and hands, rinsed out her mouth, dried her eyes and returned to her seat.

At Dylan's querying glance, she offered a wan smile. 'I'm fine now. I think.'

'Are you?'

'Not really. How about you?'

'Other than I'd like to go to the nearest bar and drink myself senseless, I'm OK, too.'

'I can't do this. I thought I could, but I can't...' Her voice faded.

'I say that myself every time I lose a patient. Sometimes our mental anesthesia just doesn't work.'

'Then why do you stay in medicine?' she asked.

'Because as tragic as cases like this one are...' he motioned in the direction of the trauma room, '...I see hundreds more where I can make a difference. The problem comes when I forget that some things simply aren't in my hands, no matter how much I wish it they were.' He leaned back and crossed his arms. 'I assume you asked that question for a reason?'

'I want to be here, yet I don't,' she said honestly. 'Sadly enough, I'm afraid if I stay my sanity will be the first to go. I'm only fooling myself and everyone else if I think otherwise.'

'You're not giving yourself enough credit, Rachel. You handled your duties like the professional that you are. As for staying, tragedy will strike whether you work here or not. Do you want to be on the outside, merely watching it happen, or do you want to wade into the middle of the fray and not let fate have the upper hand?'

Dylan's comments echoed in her mind for the rest of the afternoon and into the evening. Luckily, Nick wasn't around to see her preoccupation because he was on call and spent more time at the hospital than away from it. Beatrice Hopkins's diabetes had gone haywire; Kevin Pearson had developed a fever and a rash, which had turned out to be chickenpox; Archie McDaniel had fallen and broken his hip, and Clarence Weatherby's digoxin levels had skyrocketed when he'd forgotten his dosing schedule and had taken several more pills than had been prescribed. But it didn't stop there. Nick had his partners' patients to handle as well.

From Nick's intermittent reports and occasional phone calls, he also spent a great deal of time in the ER, and Rachel wondered if Dylan had told him about little Cassie. Since Nick hadn't mentioned that particular subject, Rachel doubted if Dylan had shared the details of either the case or their subsequent conversation. Somehow she sensed that

Dylan wouldn't say anything until she made an official announcement.

While Dylan's parting advice gave her food for thought, she mentally rehearsed her resignation letter to Theresa while she threw herself into her painting project, confident that Nick wouldn't see the preliminary stages of her decorating scheme. She was only using the basic colors for now, but once she started on the more creative work she hoped he would accept her directive that the upstairs was off-limits.

Nick came home late on Sunday evening, long after she'd washed out her paintbrushes and had showered.

'You look tired.' Seeing him as he dragged in, a full day's growth of beard on his face, she knew that now wasn't the time to broach the subject of her future at Hooper General. She pasted a smile on her face and forced a light-hearted tone in her voice.

'It's been a long two days,' he said. 'But everyone's stable and I can hand them over to my partners in the morning.'

The curtains at the kitchen window fluttered before a huge gust of wind came through and blew the newspaper off the table.

'The wind's picked up,' he said as he lowered the window.

'The weather service says a front is moving in,' Rachel said, repeating what the meteorologist had reported on the six o'clock news. 'They're only predicting a twenty per cent chance of storms for us tonight and thirty per cent for tomorrow.'

'Which means we won't see a drop of rain,' Nick commented. 'Too bad because we're overdue for moisture.' He yawned and Rachel took pity on him. He needed sleep more than he needed conversation.

'Take your shower,' she said.

He groaned. 'I'm too tired to walk across the yard.'

'Use mine,' she said, confident that he wouldn't peek at

her weekend handiwork. 'I'll have a bowl of noodle soup and chicken salad waiting for you.'

His dull eyes brightened. 'Home-made soup?'

She pretended affront. 'Is there any other kind?'

'What's for dessert?'

Because he spent more time at her house than his apartment, she'd made a point of having something sweet in the cupboard or refrigerator. 'Chocolate caramel brownies.'

He closed his eyes and patted his stomach. 'I'm in heaven. How about one of those for the road?'

'You're only going upstairs, not on a trip,' she joked, realizing that their camaraderie might come to a screeching halt once she spoke with Theresa on Monday. 'They'll be waiting for you.'

'I may fall asleep in the shower and never come back down.'

'Never fear. I'll wake you.'

'Now, *there's* a thought,' he said, leering at her. 'I see you've already freshened up.'

'About an hour ago.'

'Too bad. We could have conserved water.' His gaze grew intent as he peered at her forehead and the thin red line she saw every time she looked in a mirror. 'You took out your sutures.'

'The gash was healed so I thought I would.'

'You should have let me.'

'It wasn't a big deal, Nick. A few snips and I was done.' Rachel shooed him toward the steps. 'Now, hurry up before the phone rings again and you won't get to shower *or* eat.'

'Yes, ma'am.' He disappeared into her bedroom to retrieve the pair of shorts he slept in. Although he usually went to his own apartment to clean up, he'd used her facilities on occasion and had begun leaving extra clothes in a drawer that she'd designated for his use. Their arrangement worked out well for times such as this.

She heard the water running overhead and smiled a bitter-sweet smile, imagining his surprise if she accepted his invitation to join him. What would it hurt if she pretended for a few more hours that everything was fine and that a glorious future awaited them? He'd learn soon enough of her resignation which would go into effect as soon as Theresa found an agency nurse to take her place.

Rachel expected him to be unhappy with the news, but surely he wouldn't hold her decision against her. It wasn't as if she hadn't tried to step back into nursing. If nothing else, she deserved an A for effort even if it had ended in what Nick would consider failure.

Ironically enough, his opinion mattered a great deal to her, but she couldn't go to work and wonder if this was the day she'd lose a patient or someone she loved. Her courage, she'd discovered, was in short supply.

If he loved her as much as he claimed, then he'd accept her limitations. If he didn't…then her life would change drastically once again. Oh, they'd work together until they completed the house, but tension would replace the relaxed atmosphere.

To add insult to injury, he'd find another woman to bring home to this place—one who would be as strong and as confident as Nick himself. It wouldn't matter that Rachel had emotionally poured herself into every nook and cranny, just as she'd physically stamped her presence with every roll of paper she hung. The *other* woman's children would race through the rooms, slide down the bannister and play in the yard.

What had she told Mrs Jones? To never give up hope? In Rachel's case, she clutched it with both hands and wouldn't let go until Nick himself pried it loose. Shaking off her maudlin thoughts, she heated the soup and arranged his salad on a plate.

The water continued to run for several more minutes— long enough for her to grow concerned. She had reached the bottom step when the water stopped and she paused in case it started again. A few minutes later, Nick came down, looking far too sexy in his athletic shorts for her peace of mind. The muscles in his thighs played as he descended and she forced herself to meet his gaze rather than fix her attention on his long legs.

'I wondered if you'd developed gills,' she said, seeing his wet hair plastered to his head and his clean-shaven face.

'Not quite,' he said. 'I think I dozed off for a while, though.'

'I was about to send the cavalry.'

He met her at the bottom, his musky scent filling her nostrils as he stood beside her. 'Darn. I should have waited.'

'Better luck next time,' she quipped, crossing her fingers that there would *be* a next time.

'I won't forget.' He sniffed. 'Smells good in here.'

'Thanks,' she said, leading him to the table. 'Enjoy.'

He dug in as if he hadn't eaten all day. 'I didn't,' he answered when she posed the question. 'I filched a few cookies from the cafeteria, though.'

'Are your weekends on call usually like this?'

'No. Last night was a full moon.' He spoke as if the statement explained everything, and in a way it did. Emergency rooms and maternity wings did a booming business during this particular time in the moon's cycle. She'd seen more violence during those days as people simply lost control of their emotions and their good sense.

He reached for his brownie and gobbled it in two bites. A chocolate crumb hung on his chin and she reached across to brush it away. 'Got any more of those?' he asked.

'Yes. Want one?'

'After I read the paper.'

'I moved it to the coffee-table,' she told him, rising to clear away his dishes. 'I'll take care of these before I join you.'

Ten minutes later, Rachel strolled into the living room and found him asleep in the easy chair, the evening news-paper steepled over his midsection.

She gently lifted the paper and folded it as noiselessly

as possible. He hadn't stirred, so she leaned over him to brush at the lock of hair that fell across his forehead.

Again he didn't move and she grew bolder. She pressed her mouth to his and tasted the chocolate and caramel on his lips as she breathed in his unique scent.

'I'm awake,' he said sleepily.

'No, you're not,' she said. 'It's time for bed.'

'I'm fine right here.'

'Come on,' she said, tugging him to his feet. 'You deserve a real mattress.'

His failure to reply with a snappy comeback only indicated to her how very exhausted he was. She led him straight to her bed, determined that the lumpy sofa wasn't the place for him to catch up on his rest.

'I'll see you in the morning.'

He mumbled something she didn't quite understand. Whatever it was, it couldn't have been important because the moment his head touched the pillow he became completely oblivious to the world.

'Goodnight, sweet prince,' she murmured as she flicked off the light. As the shadows played across his face, the urge to remain grew strong. He'd never know she'd stayed with him, she decided, because he normally didn't wake up before she did. Add two sleepless nights to that equation and he wouldn't tonight either.

No, she decided. Even lying beside him under the most innocent of conditions would only pour salt into an open wound. She might want whatever crumbs she could get on what could easily be their last night together, but crumbs only made one's cravings worse. It would be easier to forget the forbidden fruit she had never tasted than to forget the fruit that she had.

Rachel grabbed an extra pillow and fresh sheet, went to the sofa and dreamed of Nick. Seemingly only minutes later, a discordant noise woke her. Her watch showed five a.m., so they'd had a fair amount of sleep, but it took her several seconds to realize that Nick's pager on the table had gone off.

She followed the noise to find it and turn off the sound. She stumbled toward the light switch, blinked owlishly as her eyes adjusted, and recognized the hospital number on the display. Disappointed over his interrupted rest, she padded into the bedroom.

'Nick?' she said softly, his skin warm under her hand as she nudged his shoulder.

He sat bolt upright, nearly knocking his head on her chin in the process. 'Yeah?'

Rachel flicked on the bedside lamp. 'You're being paged.'

'OK.' He got out of bed, frowning as if he'd just now realized where he was. 'If I slept here, where did you…?'

'We swapped places. I thought you deserved it.'

Before he could assimilate the information, she pushed him toward the kitchen phone, vowing to install an extension next to her bed. 'You'd better see what they want.'

He left and she soon heard bits and pieces of his one-sided conversation. She sat on the edge of the bed to wait, but when he reappeared with an alertness he hadn't shown earlier, she knew his day was about to begin.

'I have to go,' he said, pulling one of his spare pair of trousers out of her closet and a polo shirt from the drawer. 'ER's busy.'

'Dylan can't handle them?' she asked.

'He has six people with blunt force trauma and thinks he'll have to admit at least two.'

'An accident?'

'A fight. Have you seen my shoes?'

'The living room.'

She followed him there and watched as he tied the laces. 'So what happened? I thought fights were part of the Saturday night special. Sunday evenings are supposed to be quiet.'

'It only takes the right incentive, and they found it in

alcohol. Two started arguing and apparently they all got in the spirit of things, using anything and everything they could grab.' He rose, completely dressed. 'I'm off.'

'I'll see you in a few hours.'

He planted a quick kiss on her mouth. 'Probably so.'

At six forty-five, Rachel reported for duty. Nick was still there, suturing the last of the men's injuries. Dylan looked totally rumpled and his face exhibited a significant amount of early morning stubble.

'I hear you've had a busy night.'

Dylan snorted. 'Plain crazy is what it was.'

Rachel glanced around the ER, noticing how the night nurse was helping Nick and the trauma rooms looked as if the rapid-moving storm front in the area had somehow blown through their department. 'So I see.'

'I'm going to take a shower, eat some of those rubber eggs the hospital serves for breakfast and drink a gallon of fresh coffee,' Dylan said. 'Nick will cover for me.'

'I thought your shift ended this morning.'

'Normally it does, but the guy who's supposed to be here had a death in the family this weekend. I told them I'd stay two more days until he was free.'

'You're a pushover, Dylan Gower,' she teased.

He flashed a tired grin. 'Don't tell anybody.'

'Go on,' she said, waving him toward the door. 'Someone has to start cleaning up the mess you left and it looks as if it will be me.'

Over the next thirty minutes, she remade beds, threw away the used disposables and restocked the supplies in each room. Just as she finished, Nick walked out of the private cubicle with his patient—a man in his thirties with his entire left forearm wrapped in gauze, his other arm in a sling. Between his scabbed knuckles, blackened eyes, bloodied nose, bruised cheekbones and the cuts on his face, he looked as if he'd gone ten rounds in a boxing ring. Although he was tall, and built like a boxer he also sported the beginnings of a beer belly. She suspected the ER staff saw him on a fairly regular basis.

'Call my office for an appointment to remove those stitches,' she heard Nick say. 'And in the meantime, keep away from your so-called buddies. I don't want my handi-work ruined before you heal.'

The fellow rubbed his head. 'Don't worry, Doc. I've had enough for a while.'

The patient went through the double doors to the waiting area while Nick came toward her, his face covered in a smile. 'Good morning. I see you arrived in time to see the tail end of our latest crisis in the ER.'

She motioned toward the spot where the last patient had stood. 'I shudder to think how the others look.'

'The fellow who left could be in a beauty pageant com-pared to the two upstairs with broken bones. You'd think they'd have better things to do than use each other as punching bags.'

'No kidding.'

At that moment Dylan returned, looking like a new man. He'd scraped off the dark shadow on his chin and was wearing a fresh, crisp pair of scrubs underneath a clean, unwrinkled lab coat.

'I needed that little break,' he said cheerily. 'Oh, and I saw Theresa a little bit ago. She said to tell you that she got your message and will be over as soon as she can.'

Rachel sensed Nick's mental antennae rise. 'A message for Theresa?' he asked. 'Asking for time off already?'

Rachel squared her shoulders and drew a deep breath. 'I can't do this any more, Nick. I tried, but it's not working.'

A muscle worked in his jaw. 'You haven't even given yourself a week.'

'I don't have to,' she said. 'Maybe Dylan has already told you. A three-year-old fell in a pool on Friday and we couldn't save her. I won't put myself through that anguish any more.'

'When were you going to tell me? After you'd made the arrangements?'

'You weren't home this weekend. When was I supposed to talk to you?'

'There was plenty of time.'

'When?' she demanded. 'When you dragged yourself in at night, barely able to keep your eyes open long enough to crawl into bed? Or right before you left on your next call?'

'What about our deal?' he asked.

She'd forgotten about their compromise. 'It's over.'

'A deal is a deal.'

'I shouldn't have made it in the first place.'

Nick's face grew cold. 'For as long as I've known you, if anyone, myself included, ever tried to stop you from doing whatever you wanted, you dug in your heels to prove them wrong. I should have told you that you *couldn't* handle nursing. You might have stuck it out to prove me wrong.'

'What do you want from me?' she cried.

'I want you to let go of Grace and Molly and everyone else who's holding you back. They're ruling your life, and the sad thing is they're *dead*.'

Rachel was too stunned to reply. Instead, she watched him turn his back, take several steps and then retrace them.

'I never thought you were a quitter.'

'I'm not,' she protested, feeling the pain of his rejection.

'Really? What do you call it? There were three or four other people who also dealt with that child. I don't see them lining up to submit their resignations.' At her pause, he pressed on. 'Do you?'

Her eyes burned with unshed tears. 'No.'

'If everyone quit when he lost a patient, there wouldn't be a hospital for people to go to or staff to tend them if they managed to get there. It's easy to run away but it's harder to stand and fight. If you want to quit, then quit. If you want your memories to destroy you, like they did my father, then let them. Just don't expect to get my blessing.'

He stormed through the private staff entrance, allowing a huge gust of wind to blow in as he left. The fury of the weather seemed appropriate, considering how perfectly it reflected his mood.

'I'm sorry, Rachel,' Dylan apologized. 'I shouldn't have said anything.'

'You didn't know,' she said dully, wondering how long it would take her to get over loving Nick.

'He'll calm down.'

Rachel doubted it. Once Nick washed his hands of a situation, he didn't change his mind. 'No, he won't. You see, I was afraid he might react like this, but I'd hoped he loved me enough...' She never should have let herself believe otherwise. It made this argument all the more painful.

She cleared her throat and played with the pens in her pocket. 'You know Nick. He never has tolerated failure and in his opinion I've failed.'

'He doesn't want you to end up like his father. Granted, you're not suicidal, but you're wasting your potential.'

Raising her hands to stop him from speaking, she said, 'There are other careers just as fulfilling. He's especially upset because I made my choice without his input. He has all the answers, or so he believes.' She hated hearing the bitter note in her voice.

'He's upset because he knows what a fine nurse you are,' Dylan corrected her. 'The real tragedy is not that we'll lose a few patients during our careers. The tragedy lies in not using your talent.'

She rolled her eyes. 'You two sound alike. Did you read the same instruction manual?'

'If we sound alike, it's because we're telling you the honest truth. Sure, it's tough when we lose the Cassies of the world. All the more reason for you to be comforted by the fact that you did everything you could.' His voice grew softer. 'Quitting won't bring any of them back. Our only options are to perfect our skills so the next little Cassie won't die and to remember that we can't change certain laws of nature.'

Bonnie hurried around the corner, her eyes wide. 'I just heard. We're under a severe storm warning with wind gusts up to eighty miles an hour.'

Immediately, they heard a crash on the roof, followed by a snap as loud as a gunshot. Bonnie rushed to the private entrance and looked out. 'The hospital sign just blew off,' she said in awe.

A voice came over the public address system, announcing the weather warning and advising that no one leave the building. Bonnie unearthed the small transistor radio from their supply closet and set it on the counter while Dylan raised the volume of their police radio in time to hear reports of damage. Broken windows, signs torn off their moorings, and tree limbs snapping like twigs were only a few of the things mentioned. One newsman reported how the storm cell contained microbursts—small bursts of wind that were powerful enough to cause tornado-like damage in an area without warning.

When the police dispatcher sent fire trucks to a convenience store within a mile of the hospital because the support for the roof over the pumping station had collapsed, breaking the pumps and spilling fuel onto the street, Rachel realized how their part of town seemed to be bearing the brunt of the storm. Nick's office was only a block away from the gas station and she hoped he'd arrived safely.

'We'd better prepare for patients,' Dylan said. 'With the wind this strong, we could see all kinds of trauma, especially if a spark lands on that gasoline.'

Rachel and Bonnie hurriedly checked their supplies. Satisfied that they were ready, Rachel called Nick's apartment, her home and finally his office. 'I'm sorry, but Dr Sheridan hasn't arrived yet,' his receptionist said.

'Do you know where he is?'

'I presume he's on his way. Would you like me to page him?'

'Please, do,' she said crisply. 'Have him call the ER and ask for Rachel.' Although she was tempted to look for him, she knew her duty lay right where she was.

Within the next hour victims started to arrive, both by private car and by ambulance. Their injuries ranged from embedded glass and cuts to those who'd suffered broken bones and concussions from flying debris.

'Does this kind of weather happen often?' she asked Dylan while he sutured a scalp wound on an elderly gentleman.

'More often than we'd like,' he said. 'You'd think folks would start carrying hard hats in their cars.'

'Isn't that the truth?' their patient said. 'I've lived here all my life, but these last few years I've seen the weather do more crazy things than ever.'

Bonnie came to the door and beckoned Rachel into the hall. 'We're getting a lady who was at the convenience store. ETA is two minutes.'

'We'll put her in Two.'

The fifty-year-old woman in a neck brace and backboard to immobilize her spine was the store's manager. She had difficulty breathing in spite of receiving oxygen, and she had multiple cuts and bruises over her body.

'Flail chest,' Dylan diagnosed as they observed how a portion of her ribs moved in the opposite direction from the rest of the chest wall as she inhaled and exhaled. 'I want blood gases and a set of films, starting with a chest X-ray.'

Rachel knew that a flail chest involved a fracture of several adjacent ribs in two or more places. The danger came about from the hypoxia or oxygen deficiency in the tissues which developed as a result of the pulmonary bruising.

She badgered the radiology staff to hurry and soon they'd snapped the films confirming Dylan's assessment. The woman's oxygen saturation levels were low so she was admitted to ICU until either her condition stabilized or the surgeon decided to intervene.

In spite of the hubbub around her, Rachel couldn't get her mind off Nick. She passed by the desk where a clerk had been drafted to man the telephones and asked for the twentieth time, 'Has Dr Sheridan called yet?'

As before the girl shook her head and Rachel tried to ignore her growing sense of unease. Nick might not wish to speak with her, but he wouldn't ignore his pager.

'I'm worried about Nick,' she confessed to Dylan during a rare moment between patients.

'He still hasn't checked in?'

She shook her head. 'It's been almost two hours.'

'He's probably having phone trouble, but if we haven't heard from him by the time we finish this next case, I'll send the police after him.'

Although Theresa had pulled three nurses from other areas to help with triage, Rachel was still amazed at how fast the injured accumulated. They all took second place, however, when the ambulance discharged the next victim.

'Blunt abdominal trauma,' the EMT reported. 'We found him buried under the wreckage near those gas pumps. His BP is ninety over sixty. Pulse is one hundred.'

The man's abdomen, especially both left and right upper quadrants, was purple from bruises. 'I want a CBC, type and cross-match for four units, liver enzymes, BUN and creatinine, serum amylase and electrolytes,' Dylan ordered. 'And a urinalysis to rule out any kidney or urinary tract damage.'

Because the patient didn't respond, Rachel leaned over to inspect the cuts on his head. A familiar lock of hair caught her eye and she gasped as she recognized the face covered by the mask.

'It's Nick!'

CHAPTER ELEVEN

A MENTAL picture of Grace and Molly superimposed itself on Rachel's view of Nick lying on the stretcher. A chill slithered down her spine and spread its cold fingers through her until her fear tasted bitter in her mouth and horror sapped her breath.

No, she protested inwardly as she forcibly discarded the vision. The person lying before her was Nick. Not Grace, not Molly. Nick didn't have obvious head trauma, gaping holes in his chest and blood pouring out faster than they could pump it in. She would not give up.

Nick needed her.

She compelled herself to be objective as each team member, herself included, reported the vital signs he or she had taken. His internal injuries were serious but, unlike Grace and Molly, Nick had a fighting chance. She would make him pull through even if she had to wrestle the demons at hell's door to do so.

Empowered by her resolve, Rachel practically yelled in his ear. 'Nick. Can you hear me?'

His eyelids fluttered. 'Wh-what?'

'Can you hear me, Nick?' She fluttered over him, running her hands through his hair to check for any lumps or other cuts that might account for his slow response.

'Yeah.' He groaned. 'Don't…want…you…here.'

Rachel reeled from his declaration as if she'd been physically slapped. Then anger took hold. 'Too bad, Nick Sheridan,' she retorted. 'I'm staying so don't waste your breath arguing. Tell us where it hurts.'

'Here.' He feebly moved his hand to the left upper quadrant where the bruising appeared the most intense.

'You're going to be fine,' she told him fiercely.

He seemed to lapse back into his semi-conscious state. 'I'm cold.'

'BP is dropping,' Bonnie said.

Rachel felt his hands and arms, noting their paleness and slow capillary refill. 'He's going into shock. Stay with me, Nick.'

'Start another saline line with a large-bore needle,' Dylan ordered. 'Draw those labs now and hang a unit as soon as the blood is ready. Then get Radiology here on the double. I want a CT scan as soon as he's stable.'

Rachel worked feverishly to follow Dylan's commands, keeping a close watch on Nick's BP as their measures to raise his blood pressure took effect. She couldn't let him slip away; she wouldn't.

The thirty or so minutes for the CT scan stretched interminably, and she contacted the lab every ten minutes for Nick's results although she knew the techs weren't happy with her constant calls. But she didn't care what they thought. Nick's life was at stake.

At long last the reports rolled in. Dylan, Tom Myles, the radiologist, and Norm Hollander, the surgeon, conferred at the foot of Nick's bed while Rachel lingered. Leaving Nick for any reason was unthinkable.

'His spleen needs to come out,' Norm said, pointing to the series of pictures. 'I thought the bleeding might stop, but the damage is too extensive. His liver has a few tears but, according to these pictures, it doesn't look bad and may seal itself. I'll decide what to do when I get in there.'

'We'll send him up,' Dylan said.

Rachel grabbed Nick's hand. 'We're taking you to surgery to fix a few things.'

He licked his lips and stared at her. 'You're here. Thought I was dreaming.'

'You're not.'

'Go…away.'

The pain of hearing his rejection a second time didn't

lessen. 'You're repeating yourself, but now you're at my mercy,' she said, hardening her voice to hide her misery. 'So listen up, Nick Sheridan. Don't you dare die on me. I'll never forgive you if you do.'

The corners of his mouth twitched. 'I won't. What about…other people…?'

'They're going to be fine. Just like you are.'

He squeezed her hand in reply.

Although the wind subsided, it was some time before the influx of the injured slowed to a trickle. Rachel gratefully handed over the reins to her replacement on the incoming shift and took the stairs two at a time to reach the surgical waiting room. There, she thumbed through magazines that didn't hold her interest, paced, drank coffee and called her grandparents. After telling them to stay home because she would phone as soon as he was out of the OR, she selected another magazine.

Nick had to recover. If she'd thought losing Grace had affected her life, losing Nick would destroy it.

In that instant, she finally accepted what her subconscious and everyone else had tried to get across to her. Grace and Molly hadn't died because of her. They'd died because their bodies had been injured beyond repair. Her moment of hesitation hadn't mattered. She could lay those ghosts to rest and bury her guilt once and for all.

Now it was time to look ahead and move forward. Unfortunately, her future seemed less bright than it once had. Nick didn't want her around. If he could manage to make his wishes known while he was out of his mind with pain, then he meant every word.

Dylan strode in. 'I thought I'd find you here. Any word on Nick?'

'Not yet,' she admitted, tossing the issue of *House Beautiful* onto the table. 'I wish we'd hear something.'

'We will,' he predicted.

'I hate not knowing. At least in ER I was right there.'

Of course, if Nick had gotten his way, she wouldn't have been. The thought of standing on the other side of the glass and being relegated to the role of spectator was depressing.

Her feelings must have shown on her face because Dylan said, 'He didn't mean it.'

She shrugged and avoided his gaze. 'He did. Once he's in Recovery, I'm going home.'

'Stay with him,' he urged.

'No.' She attempted to laugh but the sound seemed more like a sob. 'He doesn't need to be upset. I don't like his decision, but I'll accept it.'

Dylan frowned but didn't comment. Finally, he said, 'You did a fine job. No one could have done better.'

His praise was more precious than an Olympic gold medal. 'I did, didn't I?' she said in some wonderment, suddenly realizing she had passed her trial by fire and mastered the fear that had paralyzed her for so long.

'Are you still thinking about turning in your resignation?'

She hadn't thought about it until now. Although Nick would undoubtedly be pleased once he heard that she'd regained her confidence, their argument had changed everything this morning. If he couldn't accept her choices, whatever they might be, their relationship didn't stand a chance.

'Yes,' she said simply. At his shocked expression, she added, 'I'm going to finish the house and go back to my old job in Wichita.' Living—and working—in Hooper wasn't an option. She glanced at her watch. 'Why is it taking so long?'

'You don't want them to rush and miss something, do you?'

'No.' She started to pace.

'Want me to check on him?'

She stopped in her tracks. 'Would you?'

He rose. 'I'll be right back.'

Before Dylan reached the door, Dr Hollander appeared,

his shirt and surgical cap wet from perspiration. 'Nick sailed through the operation. He's minus a spleen and I did a little repair work on his liver, but he'll be fine.'

Rachel's knees weakened from relief and her eyesight blurred from tears of joy. Unable to contain herself, she turned to Dylan and hugged him. 'He's all right,' she said inanely, releasing her grip on the ER physician who clearly hadn't minded her impulsive action.

Dylan smiled. 'I heard.'

'He'll be in Recovery for a few hours and then he'll spend the night in ICU,' Hollander said. 'I figure since he's one of our own, we'll give him the royal treatment. Not that he hasn't gotten it already. Between all the physicians that were crowded into the OR, I almost didn't have room for my nurses.'

'Then his partners know he's out of commission?' she asked.

'Do they know?' Hollander chuckled. 'I had to ask them to move out of my light more than once. If all those pairs of eyes missed anything, I'll eat my cap. If you want to sit with him in Recovery, be my guest.'

'Thank you,' she said, knowing her visit would be short.

'He'll be in the hospital until we're sure his liver is healing. Once he goes home, he won't be allowed to do any lifting.'

She doubted if Nick would let her oversee his recovery, but she held the thought to herself. 'Can I see him now?'

'Sure.'

Rachel didn't waste any time. She had more important things to do than to hear Hollander recite a blow-by-blow account of the procedure. Dylan could hear those gory details and pass them along later. For now, she wanted to touch Nick and to see with her own eyes that he had survived. Then she'd do as he'd asked and walk out of his life. It seemed pointless to tell him how much she loved him now.

She headed straight for the recovery room located

through the double doors adjacent to the operating suites. Although she knew what to expect and had the surgeon's reassurances of how well he was doing, she still felt a moment's trepidation at the sight of his body swathed in bandages. Tubes of all sizes connected him to a variety of bags and bottles. A variety of other lines led to the monitor above his bed so that his nurse could watch for the most minute changes in his status.

She approached the bed. 'Hi,' she said.

'You…didn't…leave.' His voice was hoarse.

'I said I wouldn't,' she said lightly to cover her hurt. 'Go to sleep. You're doing fine.'

'So…sorry…for what…I said.'

She wondered which conversation he was referring to. 'Don't apologize. You were honest.'

'Stay,' he commanded.

Rachel froze, certain at first she'd misheard him. 'You want me to stay with you?'

'Yes. I didn't want you there…in case things went bad. I didn't want you…to feel guilty.'

Tears burned in her eyes and her contacts swam. She'd completely misunderstood him. To think he'd worried more about her than himself… 'Oh, Nick.'

'I love you.' The words were faint, as if he was struggling to find enough strength to say them.

'Oh, Nick,' she said again, raising his hand to her mouth as the moisture brimmed in her eyes and tears of joy slipped down her face. 'I love you, too.'

Two days later, Nick was sitting up in his hospital bed, picking at his meal tray. 'Can't you sneak me something edible?'

Rachel studied the vegetable soup and the gelatin cubes in front of him. 'What's wrong with what you have?'

'Nothing, but I'd like to use my teeth before they forget what they're supposed to do.'

'I'm sure Dr Hollander will change your diet soon. Be patient.'

'It's hard. How's the house coming?'

'It isn't,' she said. 'Between working and spending most of my free time with you, the house has moved to the bottom of my priority list.'

'Are you sure that nursing is what you want to do?' he asked, his gaze intent. 'You're not agreeing because I lost my temper or because you bargained with The Man Upstairs?'

She grinned. 'I was too busy yelling at you to make any deals with the heavenly hosts. I'm going back to what I know.'

'I'm glad. No more guilt?'

'No more guilt where Grace and Molly are concerned,' she stated. 'I'm sure certain cases will always bother me, especially where kids are involved, but I can't do any more than my best. Maybe someday medicine will allow us to save the Graces and Mollys and Cassies.'

'I hope so,' he said. 'I'm really sorry for being so harsh with you that morning.'

'Hey,' she said. 'We just said "no more guilt," remember? It's time for a new beginning. The only memories I want controlling me are the good ones.'

Nick grinned. 'I'm sure we can work on those.'

'FYI, though,' she warned. 'I'm cutting back to part time after Merrilee returns. We have a house to finish.'

'If we hire out some of the work, we could be done by the first of October.'

'We won't stay in our budget,' she warned. 'I didn't realize we were in a hurry.'

Nick shrugged. 'I wasn't before, but I am now. I thought we could hold our wedding there.'

Her jaw dropped. 'Our wedding?'

'It seems like a nice place to have one. That is, if you want to.'

Having always seen a totally confident Nick, she found

his uncertainty endearing. 'We'll probably have a lot of differences of opinion,' she cautioned, although she wanted to shout for joy. 'You'd better be sure you can live with that.'

'I can handle it if you can.'

She flung her arms around his neck and carefully hugged him. 'What do you know? This is one idea you've had that I can't argue with.'

The week after they returned from their honeymoon in Hawaii, Rachel handed Nick a crowbar and a hammer.

'What's this for?' he asked.

'Your post honeymoon project,' she informed him. 'We've turned this place inside out over the past few months and yet we've never fixed these squeaky floorboards. It's time.'

'All right,' he said. 'By the way, have I ever told you how much I like the wallpaper?'

'More than once.' In actuality, she doubted if she'd ever tire of hearing his compliments. She'd chosen deep, rich colors to use in every room and a pattern of wispy, multicolored paint strokes trailed through the hallways. Although she'd chosen a miniature leaf pattern instead of the jungle print in their bedroom, she'd purchased a small ceramic lion to stand guard on the curio shelf. For their second anniversary, she'd add to their animal collection.

Nick crouched over the section of wooden flooring in question and Rachel peered over his shoulder. 'Do you know what you need to do?'

'Yes, but if I don't, I'm sure you'll tell me.'

'Very funny,' she said, placing a hand on his back. After his close brush with death a few months ago, she couldn't keep from reassuring herself that this—their life together—was real.

He wedged the tip of the crowbar into the space between two boards and gently pried.

'Careful.'

'I'm trying.'

The first board came up easily, as did the second. Rachel watched Nick reach into the space to check the joists. His hand froze and a strange expression came over his face.

'What's wrong?'

'There's something in here.'

She thought of a mouse and shuddered. 'Nothing dead, I hope.'

'No. It's a box.'

'A box?' Excitement filled her. 'Pull it up.'

'Hang on. It's heavy.'

Rachel waited with bated breath as Nick slowly lifted a metal strong box out of the dark hole and set it on the floor. It was covered in dust and had a padlock threaded through the latch.

'The lady *did* bury her treasure here,' she breathed. 'Can you open it?'

'Do you have a key?'

Rachel remembered the ring her grandmother had given her on the first day she'd moved to Hooper. It supposedly held every key—some new and some very old—that belonged to the house. 'Wait a minute. I'll check.'

She bounded down the stairs, grabbed the keyring from the junk drawer in the kitchen and rushed back to Nick. 'Grandpa labeled all the keys, but there was one without a tag. I asked him what it was for but he didn't know and couldn't bear to throw it away because it was old and looked unique.' She passed it to Nick. 'Try it.'

Years of dust and rust had made the turning mechanism stiff, but after he'd wiggled the key several times the lock sprang free.

Rachel felt like dancing for joy. 'This is so exciting,' she said, unable to contain herself. 'Wait! Don't lift the lid yet.'

Nick stared at her as if she'd lost her mind. 'Why not?'

'First you have to guess what might be inside.'

'Good heavens, Rachel. How do I know what someone

over a hundred years ago might have thought important enough to save for a rainy day?'

She held down the lid. 'Guess.'

He shrugged. 'Money. Gold and silver coins.'

'I choose jewelry. Precious gems.' She glanced at the diamonds embedded in the band circling her finger.

Nick grinned at her. 'May I open it now?' She lifted her hand and he raised the lid.

Rachel stared at the contents, her mouth agape. Instead of shiny coins or the sparkle of gems, an oilskin pouch lay inside.

Nick reached in and unwound the flap. Peering at its contents, he laughed.

'What is it?'

He pulled out a handful of Confederate bills. 'I presume your ancestors thought the South would win. Unfortunately, they were wrong.'

Rachel sat back on her heels to stare incredulously at the legendary Boyd treasure. 'I don't believe it.'

'Are you disappointed that we didn't find riches beyond compare hidden in the house?'

She smiled at him. 'Oh, but I did.'

'Are you holding out on me?' Nick playfully growled as he lowered her to the floor where he proceeded to kiss her. 'What treasure did you find?'

Rachel gazed into his eyes and let the love she felt for him shine brightly. 'I found you.'

Modern Romance™
...seduction and
passion guaranteed

Tender Romance™
...love affairs that
last a lifetime

Medical Romance™
...medical drama on
the pulse

Historical Romance™
...rich, vivid and
passionate

Sensual Romance™
...sassy, sexy and seductive

27 new titles every month.

*With all kinds of Romance for
every kind of mood...*

MILLS & BOON®

Makes any time special™

MAT4RS

0702/73/MB38

Coming in July

❦❦❦

The Ultimate Betty Neels Collection

❦❦❦

* A stunning 12 book collection beautifully packaged for you to collect each month from bestselling author Betty Neels.

* Loved by millions of women around the world, this collection of heartwarming stories will be a joy to treasure forever.

2 FREE
books and a surprise gift!

We would like to take this opportunity to thank you for reading this Mills & Boon® book by offering you the chance to take TWO more specially selected titles from the Medical Romance™ series absolutely FREE! We're also making this offer to introduce you to the benefits of the Reader Service™—

- ★ FREE home delivery
- ★ FREE gifts and competitions
- ★ FREE monthly Newsletter
- ★ Exclusive Reader Service discount
- ★ Books available before they're in the shops

Accepting these FREE books and gift places you under no obligation to buy, you may cancel at any time, even after receiving your free shipment. Simply complete your details below and return the entire page to the address below. *You don't even need a stamp!*

YES! Please send me 2 free Medical Romance books and a surprise gift. I understand that unless you hear from me, I will receive 4 superb new titles every month for just £2.55 each, postage and packing free. I am under no obligation to purchase any books and may cancel my subscription at any time. The free books and gift will be mine to keep in any case.

M2ZEA

Ms/Mrs/Miss/Mr ....Initials.....................................
BLOCK CAPITALS PLEASE

Surname ....

Address ....

....

....Postcode...................................

Send this whole page to:
UK: FREEPOST CN81, Croydon, CR9 3WZ
EIRE: PO Box 4546, Kilcock, County Kildare (stamp required)